Approval

Omega Queen Series, Volume 7

W.J. May

Published by Dark Shadow Publishing, 2020.

This is a work of fiction. Similarities to real people, places, or events are entirely coincidental.

APPROVAL

First edition. November 15, 2020.

Copyright © 2020 W.J. May.

Written by W.J. May.

Also by W.J. May

Bit-Lit Series
Lost Vampire
Cost of Blood
Price of Death

Blood Red Series
Courage Runs Red
The Night Watch
Marked by Courage
Forever Night
The Other Side of Fear
Blood Red Box Set Books #1-5

Daughters of Darkness: Victoria's Journey
Victoria
Huntress
Coveted (A Vampire & Paranormal Romance)
Twisted
Daughter of Darkness - Victoria - Box Set

Great Temptation Series
The Devil's Footsteps
Heaven's Command
Mortals Surrender

Hidden Secrets Saga
Seventh Mark - Part 1
Seventh Mark - Part 2
Marked By Destiny
Compelled
Fate's Intervention
Chosen Three
The Hidden Secrets Saga: The Complete Series

Kerrigan Chronicles
Stopping Time
A Passage of Time
Ticking Clock
Secrets in Time
Time in the City
Ultimate Future

Mending Magic Series
Lost Souls
Illusion of Power
Challenging the Dark

Castle of Power
Limits of Magic
Protectors of Light

Omega Queen Series
Discipline
Bravery
Courage
Conquer
Strength
Validation
Approval
Blessing

Paranormal Huntress Series
Never Look Back
Coven Master
Alpha's Permission
Blood Bonding
Oracle of Nightmares
Shadows in the Night
Paranormal Huntress BOX SET

Prophecy Series
Only the Beginning
White Winter
Secrets of Destiny

Revamped Series
Hidden
Banished
Converted

Royal Factions
The Price For Peace
The Cost for Surviving
The Punishment For Deception
The Most Cherished
The Strength to Endure

The Chronicles of Kerrigan
Rae of Hope
Dark Nebula
House of Cards
Royal Tea
Under Fire
End in Sight
Hidden Darkness
Twisted Together
Mark of Fate
Strength & Power
Last One Standing
Rae of Light
The Chronicles of Kerrigan Box Set Books # 1 - 6

The Chronicles of Kerrigan: Gabriel
Living in the Past
Present For Today
Staring at the Future

The Chronicles of Kerrigan Prequel
Christmas Before the Magic
Question the Darkness
Into the Darkness
Fight the Darkness
Alone in the Darkness
Lost in Darkness
The Chronicles of Kerrigan Prequel Series Books #1-3

The Chronicles of Kerrigan Sequel
A Matter of Time
Time Piece
Second Chance
Glitch in Time
Our Time
Precious Time

The Hidden Secrets Saga
Seventh Mark (part 1 & 2)

The Kerrigan Kids
School of Potential
Myths & Magic
Kith & Kin
Playing With Power
Line of Ancestry
Descent of Hope
Illusion of Shadows
Frozen by the Future

The Queen's Alpha Series
Eternal
Everlasting
Unceasing
Evermore
Forever
Boundless
Prophecy
Protected
Foretelling
Revelation
Betrayal
Resolved
The Queen's Alpha Box Set

The Senseless Series
Radium Halos - Part 1
Radium Halos - Part 2

Nonsense
Perception
The Senseless - Box Set Books #1-4

Standalone
Shadow of Doubt (Part 1 & 2)
Five Shades of Fantasy
Zwarte Nevel
Shadow of Doubt - Part 1
Shadow of Doubt - Part 2
Four and a Half Shades of Fantasy
Dream Fighter
What Creeps in the Night
Forest of the Forbidden
Arcane Forest: A Fantasy Anthology
The First Fantasy Box Set

Watch for more at www.wjmaybooks.com.

OMEGA QUEEN SERIES
APPROVAL

USA Today Bestselling Author

W.J. MAY

Copyright 2020 by W.J. May

THIS E-BOOK OR PRINT is licensed for your personal enjoyment only. This e-book/paperback may not be re-sold or given away to other people. If you would like to share this book with another person, please purchase an additional copy for each recipient. If you're reading this book and did not purchase it, or it was not purchased for your use only, then please return to Smashwords.com and purchase your own copy. Thank you for respecting the hard work of the author.

All rights reserved. No part of this publication may be reproduced, stored in or introduced into a retrieval system, or transmitted, in any form, or by any means (electronic, mechanical, photocopying, recording, or otherwise) without the prior written permission of both the copyright owner and the above publisher of this book.

This is a work of fiction. Names, characters, places, brands, media, and incidents are either the product of the author's imagination or are used fictitiously. Any resemblance to actual person, living or dead, events, or locales is entirely coincidental. The author acknowledges the trademarked status and trademark owners of various products referenced in this work of fiction, which have been used without permission. The publication/use of these trademarks is not authorized, associated with, or sponsored by the trademark owners.

All rights reserved.
Copyright 2020 by W.J. May
Approval, Book 7 of the Omega Queen Series
Cover design by: Book Cover by Design

No part of this book may be used or reproduced in any manner whatsoever without written permission, except in the case of brief quotations embodied in articles and reviews.

Have You Read the C.o.K Series?

The Chronicles of Kerrigan
Book I - *Rae of Hope* is FREE!

BOOK TRAILER:
http://www.youtube.com/watch?v=gILAwXxx8MU

How hard do you have to shake the family tree to find the truth about the past?

Fifteen year-old Rae Kerrigan never really knew her family's history. Her mother and father died when she was young and it is only when she accepts a scholarship to the prestigious Guilder Boarding School in England that a mysterious family secret is revealed.

Will the sins of the father be the sins of the daughter?

As Rae struggles with new friends, a new school and a star-struck forbidden love, she must also face the ultimate challenge: receive a tattoo on her sixteenth birthday with specific powers that may bind her to an unspeakable darkness. It's up to Rae to undo the dark evil in her family's past and have a ray of hope for her future.

Find W.J. May

Website:
https://www.wjmaybooks.com
Facebook:
https://www.facebook.com/pages/Author-WJ-May-FAN-PAGE/141170442608149
Newsletter:
SIGN UP FOR W.J. May's Newsletter to find out about new releases, updates, cover reveals and even freebies!
http://eepurl.com/97aYf

Approval Blurb:

USA Today Bestselling author, W.J. May, continues the highly anticipated bestselling YA/NA series about love, betrayal, magic and fantasy.
Be prepared to fight... it's the only option.
You cannot hide from destiny... It will always find you.

When Evie and her friends take an unexpected detour, they find themselves face to face with the last person they ever imagined they'd find—the very witch who delivered the fateful prophecy all those years ago. Relief is short-lived, as the woman provides more questions than answers—sending them each down a path of discovery. But there's no telling if they'll like what they find.

Danger lurks around every corner. A journey home becomes a matter of life or death. The Dunes await but chaos is already upon them, ripping asunder the very fabric of the realm.

Is there a way to stop it?

Or has it always been a matter of fate?

BE CAREFUL WHO YOU trust. Even the devil was once an angel.

The Queen's Alpha Series

Eternal
Everlasting
Unceasing
Evermore
Forever
Boundless
Prophecy
Protected
Foretelling
Revelation
Betrayal
Resolved

The Omega Queen Series

Discipline
Bravery
Courage
Conquer
Strength
Validation
Approval
Blessing
Balance
Grievance
Enchanted
Gratified

Chapter 1

"You are a truly abysmal guide."

The six friends were frozen very still, staring bracingly at the ancient woman waving them closer from the bank of the river. It wouldn't have seemed so ominous if the boat wasn't drifting closer of its own accord. It wouldn't have seemed so ominous if the woman hadn't been a witch. It also wouldn't have seemed so ominous if she'd been in possession of more than half her teeth.

Asher shot Ellanden a quick look, muttering under his breath. "Be fair. Are you really going to blame this on the shifter?"

The fae kept his eyes locked on the woman, speaking without moving his lips. "You'll find there's no shortage of things I can blame on the shifter. But since he was the one paddling the boat—*yes*. I believe this falls squarely on him."

Evie smacked him in the chest, eyes glowing with excitement. "Don't be ridiculous! This woman gave me the *prophecy*. It doesn't matter how we ended up in this part of the river—we were clearly meant to come!"

"*Meant* to come?" the fae echoed, forcing his eyes away from the witch's dilapidated hut long enough to shoot her a disbelieving glare. "I'm not going in there!"

Cosette stared down at the boat, propelling towards the shore all by itself. "I'm not sure we have much of a choice..."

"Seth, turn this monstrosity around!" Ellanden commanded.

"You're not going in there?" Evie quoted icily, hoping very much the woman was hard of hearing, as her friend was famously rude. "On what *possible* grounds are you—"

"What possible grounds?" he hissed, drawing himself to a more impressive height. "Let me spell it out for you, princess, and fear not, I will make myself clear. I'm not trusting some kindly old magician. I'm not sitting down for supper and drinking the tea. I'm not waking up in a cage, only to find I'm not actually awake at all, and I'm not going to end up chained to a dog-post in the backyard, splashing in the mud, while secretly bleeding out between my ribs! I am *not* going inside!"

The rest of them stared at him a moment before Asher gestured to the swamp.

"Ellanden, don't be silly. There is no backyard."

"Quite right," Evie agreed briskly as the fae dropped his face into his hands. "Besides, you're basically paralyzed. You have very little say in where you'll be going."

"What was that?" The witch cupped a hand over her ear. "I couldn't quite hear you!"

"Thanks for the invite, but not today!" Ellanden waved cordially, reaching for an oar. "We're actually on a bit of a schedule—"

"Would you *stop*?" Evie smacked him again, ignoring the agonizing wince. "You know just as well as me we were brought here for a reason. You need to trust the fates."

He shot her a dry look. "Our fates seem to have a dark sense of humor."

She offered a sweet smile. "*Yours* would."

All the while, the boat continued its slow journey—taking them further away from the river and deeper into the mist. When the trailing branches of a cypress pulled back like a curtain, beckoning them inside, Ellanden reached back to grab the shifter, whispering urgently under his breath.

"I don't care if you have to jump in and swim—get us back to the river."

Seth gestured helplessly to the boat. "What would you have me do?" he muttered, shooting a glance at the witch. "It's moving against the current."

Ellanden clenched his jaw, trying not to panic as they neared the shore. "Fine. I'll do it myself."

"Is that a crocodile?" Asher asked casually.

The fae twisted around as much as he was able, scanning the muddy banks. After a few tense seconds, he glanced suspiciously back at the vampire.

"Did you really see a crocodile, or are you just trying to keep me in the boat?"

"Must have been fifty-feet long..."

"Throw me the rope," the witch called, lifting a pair of gnarled hands. "I'll reel you in the rest of the way."

"She'll reel us—"

"We don't have one," Evie answered apologetically. "Sorry, this was kind of a spur of the moment contraption. You see, there was this pack of demonic hyenas—"

"That's very nice, dear," the witched croaked dismissively. "I'll just do it myself."

The misty air seemed to crackle with energy as the old woman made a strange sideways gesture with her hands. At once the boat lurched forward, spilling them all to the floor.

Seven hells!

"There was no crocodile," Ellanden assured himself quietly, gripping the railing as they sliced through the water. "I can go right now—"

"This is amazing!" Freya popped up eagerly, lifting her hands as the boat jerked wildly across the cresting waves. "I'll help!"

The fae yanked her down just as fast. "You will do nothing of the sort."

But whatever other protests or escapes he had in mind, it was too late. No sooner had he grabbed Freya's cloak than the boat surged a final time, leaving the water entirely as it scraped onto the shore. There was a collective gasp, followed by a ringing silence, as they froze perfectly still.

...is it over?

With her eyes closed, Evie could almost believe she'd imagined it. That they were still drifting lazily down the river, fingers trailing in the water, slipping in and out of dreams.

Then a rasping voice crackled in her ear.

"We seem to have broken your little boat."

The friends pried open their eyes, then stared down at the giant hole in the middle of their makeshift canoe. Freya prodded at it with her toe. Ellanden looked close to tears.

The witch clapped her hands with a smile. "So who's ready for a nice cup of tea?"

IT WASN'T EASY GETTING to the old woman's house—and not just because it was tucked in a magical pocket of an endless river, that may or may not have been visible to the rest of the world.

It was also on stilts.

"I don't understand," Cosette murmured, navigating as best she could through the putrid mulch. The fae and vampire were irritatingly light-footed, while the others were up to their ankles in swamp. "She built this place—probably cloaked it as well—kept it secret, guided us here... after surviving countless extermination attempts that stretch back decades before the Great War."

She paused as a giant snake slithered across the trail.

"All that...and she's worried about flooding?"

Considering the path the friends had already travelled, the stilts seemed a particularly cruel twist. Especially given that one of their party had recently flirted with that unholy line between the living and the dead. It was a fact that left his patience in rather short supply.

"Do not look for sense in this," Ellanden hissed, clinging tightly to the side of the vampire's neck. Each step was as dizzying as it was painful, and he was keenly aware of the phosphorescent sludge seeping up the inside of his boot. "It's just the latest in a series of bad decisions brought to you by my ex-friends. The reason I hate redheads, and the moron who's dating her."

Asher shot him a sideways glance. "Would you like me to drop you?"

The fae held on tighter.

"Leave him alone," Seth murmured, hovering cautiously in the back of the group. The fae's body had been broken in rescue of the wolf, so perhaps he felt obliged to help him. But it was hard not to take him seriously when he cast a pointed glance up at the house. "It's not like he doesn't have a point. You three don't really have the best track record with that sort of thing..."

The friends sobered immediately, eyes darting around with little sparks of suspicion as the witch led them further and further into the swamp.

It wasn't far to go, but it was far to climb.

When the fae saw the ladder, he promptly closed his eyes and went limp. Asher caught him with a grin and draped him lightly over his shoulder, proceeding to make the climb with one hand.

Maybe he's right, maybe this is a mistake...

From the moment Evie's foot left the ground, she felt herself seized with the same quiet panic. Yes, she believed they'd been guided there for a reason. And yes, she'd already met the witch on one occasion before. But too many times over the course of their travels had the young friends found themselves at the mercy of some quirk of magic, hostage to powers beyond their control.

It was enough to make them ask questions, enough to make them pause. It might even have been enough to make them back turn around. But before the princess could whisper such a thing to the others she found herself at the top of the ladder, stepping slowly onto the wooden porch.

Well, this is...wonderful.

She took a step closer, eyes widening in surprise.

It would have been impossible to guess the inside of the house based upon what it looked like from the river. The princess had been prepared for a continuation of the swamp. Floorboards slick with algae, curtains rotted with mold. The desiccated remains of insects lying in strangely uniform piles, as a hundred years' worth of poisonous vines crept silently through the windows.

But the witch wasn't just hiding in the bayou. She had created a home.

Everything about it was warm. From the colors, to the clutter, to the inexplicable aroma of freshly-baked bread. There were herbs hanging in the kitchen, a fire crackling in the hearth, and tiny flowers grew in forgotten teacups that had been scattered anywhere that touched the sun.

Mugs were chipped and painted. Thick blankets had been sewn by hand.

It was everything the friends could have asked for. Everything they didn't know they'd been missing until they found themselves standing in front of it, aching to go inside.

"You live here?" Evie asked incredulously, unable to keep the surprise from her voice.

The witch glanced over her shoulder as the six friends froze in the doorway. Wide-eyed and trembling. Too cautious, too thin. So perpetually cold, they didn't realize their fingers were numb until they stepped into the glow from the hearth. She opened her mouth to say one thing, then decided on another—spreading her arms and welcoming them inside with a warm, crinkling smile.

"Home sweet home."

THE HUT WAS MUCH BIGGER than it looked from the outside. So much bigger that Evie quickly realized it must have been a spell. One side was dedicated to an open living area—complete with a kitchen, a miniature library, and a cluster of fireside chairs surrounded by shelves of books—while several smaller rooms for sleep were clustered at the end of the hall.

Evie's eyes went to them at once. Fresh pillows had been stacked by the doors.

"Well, that's a handy trick," Freya murmured, looking around in a daze.

The others were in a similar state of disorientation—staring with the slightly feral expression of children who'd been left out in the wilderness too long. They gawked at the throw rugs like they'd never seen such a thing before. Their eyes took in the scented candles and cozy armchairs, like they were waiting for monsters to crash in through the glass.

"Take off your shoes!" the witch called.

In unison, the friends looked down at their feet.

Their leather boots were coated in a strange combination of mud and swamp, mixed with a generous helping of dried blood from the fight the day before. Little pools of water trickled onto the porch as they peeled them off, hopping for balance with various degrees of difficulty.

The old woman watched with a twinkle in her eyes.

"Much better." She waved them forward, shutting the door behind them with a flick of her hand. "From a distance, you could almost pass as civilized."

Bold words from someone who spent the majority of her time in a swamp. But the friends were in no position to turn down the invitation. With a shiver they stepped over the threshold, blinking quickly as their eyes adjusted to the warm light.

"I'm sorry," Evie said suddenly, blushing with shame, "I can't remember—"

"It's Evianna," the witch replied kindly. "And don't fault yourself for not remembering. A lot's happened since the first time we met."

The princess nodded slowly as that fateful night flashed through her mind.

Too many times she'd lost herself in the memory, trying to fit the pieces back together. But it was like trying to remember a dream. She could picture herself wandering through the party, remembering how the witch had waved her into the tent. She had been unimpressed. It was a cheap carnival trick. Crystal balls and soggy tealeaves clumped at the bottom of a glass. The witch herself was an obvious fraud, with a face so old it would have been better suited as a mask.

She came up with half a dozen excuses. She prepared for a quick escape.

...then everything changed.

"I didn't think I'd see you again," she murmured, turning to face the witch for the first time.

A shiver ran through her shoulders, and she realized that from the moment they'd spotted her from the river she'd been purposely avoiding the woman's eyes. Like if she looked too long, the door might reopen. That she'd find herself facing another cosmic sentence—one she couldn't escape.

Evianna threw back her head with a burst of startling laughter. "Neither did I! Funny how these things work out, isn't it?"

The friends stared back without blinking, the same blank expression sweeping across their faces. They had been expecting some kind of divine message. A dire warning, or 'keep up the good work', or even a cosmic nudge to get them back on track. At the very least, they were expecting to have been expected. How was it possible the witch was as surprised as they were?

"What does that mean?" Asher asked softly, looking the woman up and down.

He had lowered Ellanden back to the floor, and the two of them were standing bracingly by the door. Unbeknownst to him, the fae kept sneaking one foot back onto the porch. As if hoping to thwart whatever secret time loop they might have triggered by stepping inside.

The witch's eyes crinkled with a smile. "Which part confused you, child?"

His eyes flashed quickly to Evie before returning to their strange hostess. Dilated with that same quiet intensity the others had learned to both admire and fear.

"You brought us here... What are we supposed to do now?"

Six pairs of eyes flew back across the room. Six people waited breathlessly for an answer.

But Evianna only shrugged.

"I didn't bring you here. You brought yourselves. My involvement in your story ended the moment I gave you that prophecy. Until this afternoon I thought we'd parted ways for good."

While the others were utterly bewildered, she didn't seem to mind. Quite the contrary, the woman looked as though she hadn't had company in a good long while.

"And as for what you're supposed to do now?"

Her eyes twinkled as she swept them up and down.

"Might I suggest a long bath..."

Chapter 2

As it turned out, the bath was a bit metaphorical. Nevertheless there were two massive washtubs, full to the brim with magically-heated water, and a stone-floored room clouding with steam. Too tired to be furtive the friends undressed as far as they dared, then managed as best they could with a damp towel. There were many secret grimaces, many quiet profanities as they gathered together. Cleaning methodically, peeling back the layers, and dabbing gingerly at the darker bruises and stains of blood.

They might have beat the hyenas back in the grassland, might have even survived their shipwreck in the Kreo jungle just a few days before, but they'd been sleeping under the stars for as long as they could remember, and every unscripted day had taken its toll.

Cosette closed her eyes and turned her face to the wall, biting down on her lip as she popped a bone in her shoulder back into place. Seth glanced out the window, desperate to shift to help heal his own wounds. Evie tried to gauge the bite marks in her side, wondering if they needed stitches.

Some of it was inevitable. Some of it was suffered in the protection of the others. But worse by far was the damage inflicted by each other's own hands.

Asher picked up the towel, wondering where to begin, then glanced with a hint of surprise at the twin lacerations trailing up both his wrists. He didn't remember getting them. They seemed too precise a thing for the blunt force of the hyenas. Perhaps—

His face went still and his eyes lifted slowly to Ellanden.

The fae was on the far side of the room, mothering his own wounds with uncharacteristically clumsy hands. It had been too soon to travel after his brush with death, and that haste was taking its toll. By dark coincidence he came across a similar hurt, a fracture that had come at the vampire's hands. He flexed it painfully, gripping the wall for balance, then glanced in silence across the room.

The two men locked eyes for a moment, then continued working with renewed speed.

Needless to say, it was hardly the relaxing experience the witch had intended. Quite the contrary. By the time the friends were finished everyone was feeling each hurt, fresh and raw, in a way they hadn't before. An awkward silence fell over them as they filed out into the hall.

"How many rooms are there?" Evie asked quietly.

Seth opened the doors quickly, checking to see what was inside.

"Four. These are all bedrooms."

She nodded a bit self-consciously, then without saying a word the friends paired off so that six became four. Evie and Asher would share together. So would Freya and Cosette.

"Well...that's it for me," Ellanden said with forced lightness. "If you insist we are to spend the night in a swamp, then I'm going to bed. Sleep well."

The others lifted their hands, murmuring goodnights, but just as the prince was turning to leave Asher called out to him, "Will you be all right?"

He blurted it before he could stop himself, and he clearly wanted to stop himself, but the fae hadn't been left unsupervised since that fateful moment he blinked open his eyes. Most of the time the others were watching him carefully—counting breaths and making sure he *didn't* fall asleep.

Ellanden glanced back in surprise, then nodded quickly—holding tight to the edge of the doorframe. "I'll be fine. See you in the morning."

The vampire's eyes tightened and Evie was quick to intercede.

APPROVAL

"We should stitch that up before you sleep another night." She glanced at the fresh stain of blood in his ivory hair. "It's too deep to close on its own. I'm sure the witch has something—"

"It's fine." Ellanden lifted a hand to his head, almost as if he'd forgotten. "Another night and it should be fine."

Except it doesn't work like that.

"Come on," she urged, lowering her voice, trying to sound reasonable, "let Asher stitch it up. You know he's the best with needle and thread—"

"Goodnight, Everly."

He was gone a moment later, closing the door swiftly behind him.

The rest of them stood there in awkward silence, debating the best course of action. Then Cosette crossed the hall and headed after him. "I'll stay with him until morning. Goodnight."

"Goodnight," they chanted in return.

The door closed again and the silence became even more oppressive.

Freya was staring after Ellanden, but when she saw the others watching she flushed bright red and vanished into her room. Seth glanced between the remaining two doors, looking generally troubled, then forced a quick smile and did the same. In the end it was just Evie and Asher, still damp from their attempt at a bath, frozen in a stranger's hallway, standing side by side.

She glanced up at him and he nodded quickly, pulling open the final door.

There wasn't much. Just a handful of candles and a simple bed. The window looked out over the river. The princess walked slowly towards it, gazing out at the distant waves.

"What are we doing here?" she murmured.

Asher paused in the process of turning down the bed and joined her, vanishing a moment before reappearing at her side. Two hands rested lightly upon her shoulders as he leaned down to look with her, staring silently through the glass. After a few seconds, he kissed the top of her head.

"Come to bed."

She stood there a second longer then climbed onto the mattress, pulling up the blankets as she settled back in his arms. It still felt strange to do such a thing. They'd slept together many times, but never on a proper bed. No matter how hard she tried, it was impossible to lie still.

The blankets were too soft. The pillow was dangerously inviting. Why bother with candles when they could see perfectly well by the light of the moon? She turned over several times, striking the vampire in the process, before settling exactly where she'd been before, glaring into the dark.

"...are you having a fit?"

Asher had been watching for several minutes, graciously absorbing every clumsy kick and flailing elbow with a secret smile. It was the glare that broke him, seeing the reflection in the glass.

She glanced over her shoulder, coloring with a blush. "No, sorry, it's just...is this pillow weird to you?"

It took him a second to catch up.

"The pillow?"

She punched it for good measure, trying to knock it into shape. "It's too high, right? *Abnormally* high. It keeps tilting my head at this ridiculous angle, and when my head's tilted I feel like I can't breathe."

"Why do you—"

"I just *do*, Asher." She sat up abruptly, folding her arms across her chest. "We shouldn't have taken separate rooms, anyway. We should have all stayed together."

He sat up slowly beside her, dark hair falling loose around his face. "You're worried about the witch?"

She shrugged petulantly, curling her knees into her chest.

To be honest, she wasn't worried about the witch. Not only had Evianna set them on their fateful path, but she was friends with Petra and Michael. They had sought her out before the festival at the castle. Surely there was no greater evidence that a person could be trusted.

It wasn't the witch...it was *them*.

"We're in trouble," she whispered. "Can you feel it?"

It wasn't just the fighting. Each one of them was descended from a line of fabled warriors, and there had been fights before. And it wasn't just the arguing—though that was sometimes even worse.

This was different. This went deeper.

It had started slowly, deceptively—posing as things less troubling. First indecision, then confusion, then fatigue. A question to which they should have known the answer. A lingering look after a decision had been made. Faith eroded and little cracks began to show. Before they knew it, the friends found themselves tripping over lines and problems where none had existed before.

Asher stiffened beside her, but it was nothing he hadn't been thinking himself.

"We're going to..." he started with confidence, then bowed his head with a sigh. "We'll *have* to get through it. There's no other choice."

She stared at him a second longer, then nodded quickly.

Like it was that simple. Like everything was all right.

THE PRINCESS GAZED down at the letters, shimmering in dark ink on the parchment, scrawled in a hasty, untrained hand. She recognized what each one was, but no matter how long she stood there, no matter how hard she tried, she couldn't put them together. It was as if she'd forgotten the common tongue. Those simple words she'd known since childhood blurred together in an endless jumble, stretching into the distance as far as the eye could see.

She knelt to the ground in a flicker of candlelight, touching the tips of her fingers to the page. There was truth here, hidden in plain sight.

There was illumination. The answer to a question she hadn't yet begun to frame...

Then a booming voice echoed somewhere behind her and she took off running, sucking in a frightened breath as her feet flew across the page. Faster and faster she went, afraid to look behind her, afraid to stop. Entire storylines were dissolving beneath her—flying off the paper the second her feet touched down. Horrible pictures melted into swirls of ink as the faded characters reached out to grab her, tugging at the hem of her dress, dragging her to the ground.

The clouds churned in violent colors. Peals of deafening laughter clapped across the sky.

For a split second, the words shimmered into focus. For a split second, the answer was perfectly clear.

Then fire rained down from the sky, stranding the princess in the middle of the story as the pages crumbled to smoldering ash beneath her hands.

"No!" she cried, trying to salvage whatever was left. Fragments of burning paper slipped from her fingers, charring her skin and lighting the folds of her dress on fire. "I haven't read it yet!"

The laughter rang louder, mighty wings beating through the sky.

"I don't know what it says!"

She looked towards the heavens and let out a piercing scream.

"NO!"

A gust of cold air slapped her in the face.

"Evie?"

The princess awoke to find herself standing by the open window, one foot thrown over the ledge, both hands braced against the frame. Asher was lying in bed, staring in shock.

"...what are you doing?"

She pulled in a sharp breath, glancing immediately at her thin nightdress—half-expecting to find it still on fire. The blazing inferno was gone, leaving nothing but pale sunlight as morning broke gently over the little swamp. Wisps of vapor drifted above the water and brightly-plumed birds called back and forth, shaking out their wings before lifting gracefully into the sky.

"Honey?"

She snapped back to the present, only to see the handsome vampire still watching her from the bed. For a second, she almost had to feel sorry for him. Sleep-tousled hair, saucer-like eyes. His hand was still touching the imprint on the mattress where she'd been sleeping just seconds before.

"It's nothing, I just...I just had a bad dream."

...a seriously disturbing bad dream.

...a fire and brimstone bad dream.

...again.

His lips curved with the hint of a smile as he patted the mattress beside him. She grinned bashfully and climbed up without a second thought, casting a fleeting glance back at the window.

Was I seriously going to jump?

"Let me guess..." He eased them back against the headboard, wrapping both arms around her waist. "We received some cosmic hate mail, set off on a suicide mission, ran into every monster in the five kingdoms, drifted into a magical bog, then broke our boat—stranding us forever."

She gave a shaky laugh, still trying to shake the remnants of the dream. "Don't be silly. I could never imagine something so terrible."

He shook his head with a mock frown. "Sweetheart, I have some very bad news..."

They laughed softly, but quieted almost as fast—staring at the opposite wall as their smiles faded into something rather grim. After a little while, he glanced down at the top of her head.

"Seriously...are you okay?"

She wanted to say yes. She started to say yes.

But she ended up saying something very different instead.

"What did you say to Ellanden? Right before he opened his eyes?"

The vampire had spoken so quietly there wasn't any way she could have heard him. None of the rest of them had any idea. Yet she'd somehow heard it all the same.

'It's not supposed to be you. You have to keep going. It's supposed to be me.'

Each word had been whispered, tears streaming down his face. He'd said them to Ellanden but his eyes were on the clouds, offering them up in a kind of prayer.

He tensed behind her, wishing abruptly that she hadn't asked.

"What do you mean?" he stalled. "I was...I was terrified we'd lost him. I was just asking him to wake up."

The princess twisted around, staring into his eyes. "That's all?"

He froze imperceptibly, then his brow creased with the hint of a frown. "...what did you dream?"

They stared at each other a split second.

Then a sudden shriek echoed through the house.

What the—?!

They were out of bed a second later, streaking down the hall to see Freya standing in the living room, both hands clamped over her mouth. The others were just a second behind them, each of them pausing with sudden dread before inching forward to see for themselves.

Is that—

Evianna was sprawled disjointedly over a recliner, mouth hanging wide open, eyes staring unblinkingly towards the roof. An empty bottle was clutched in one hand, while an overturned glass lay on the floor just a few feet away. The front door was loose on its hinges, creaking in the breeze.

Evie froze where she stood, all the color draining from her face.

"Is she...? Is she actually...?"

Freya shook her head quickly, eyes brimming with tears.

"I don't know," she whimpered. "I just came out here and found her like this."

The friends hesitated a moment longer, then forced themselves closer—steeling themselves with faltering breaths as they leaned forward, six faces peering down over the chair.

It was quiet a moment, nothing but pounding hearts.

Then the witch let loose a hacking cough.

The friends leapt back with a collective scream, clutching each other like they were back in the nursery, brandishing the witch's own cutlery without a hint of shame.

"Seven hells!" Asher gasped. "We thought you were dead!"

Evianna blinked in surprise, glancing around the circle.

"Dead?" she squawked before getting to her feet. "Of course I'm not dead!"

Evie lifted a hand to her chest, lowering the salad prongs she'd snatched off the table.

No, you're just nine hundred years old.

The others slowly lowered their own weapons as the woman fussed about, smoothing her dress and kicking the empty bottle of liquor under her chair.

"Dead," she repeated in a huff, shooting the vampire a reproachful look. "That's an incredibly rude thing to say to someone. Especially coming from someone like you."

Asher blushed and lowered his eyes to the floor. "Yes, ma'am."

It was the manners that softened her. Or maybe the fact that the princess of the Fae was still clutching a spoon. At any rate, the scowl soon faded into something unexpectedly warm.

"You're all looking a little better. A little cleaner, at any rate." She gestured toward the table with a lopsided smile. "How about some breakfast?"

Chapter 3

As fate would have it, the concept of 'breakfast' turned out to be as hollow as the offer of a bath. The witch stayed around just long enough to solidify the plan and confiscate any remaining flatware before pointing them toward the kitchen and announcing she was going for a walk.

The door swung shut behind her, leaving them standing in a daze.

"I don't understand," Asher murmured, staring after her. "We were standing right above her, and I swear to the heavens I couldn't hear a heartbeat. I've seen corpses more animated."

The others cast him a strange look, but Seth chuckled and moved back to the chair. With quick hands he rummaged beneath it and came up with the empty bottle, giving it a quick sniff.

"There were a few like her in my village. Same drink of choice." He glanced at the cabinets, as if there might be more. "Add on another seven thousand years..."

Evie laughed in spite of herself as the rest of them wandered to the kitchen, taking stock of the shelves to see what was there. All except one. Ellanden took a single look then wrote off the entire endeavor—hobbling back down the hallway to get more sleep. Cosette snatched a needle and thread from a sewing box by the hearth and headed after him.

The door opened and shut. Several choice profanities were soon to follow.

"Breakfast, breakfast..." Freya murmured in a sing-song voice, ignoring the violent oaths coming from the other end of the hall. "How about...biscuits!"

She popped out of the cupboard with a bright smile, holding a whisk and a pan.

"Biscuits sound great." Evie threw out a hand for balance as a distant collision shook the walls of the little house. The Fae had notoriously short tempers, especially in the morning. "I'd offer to help, but—"

"But you couldn't prepare a meal to save your life?" Freya dumped some sugar and flour into a bowl with a teasing smile. "Yes, I remember."

The windows rattled as there was another impact. This one was followed by a howl of pain.

"That's not too surprising." Seth sniffed at the air, then opened a random cabinet and pulled out a bottle that smelled of rum. He cocked a thumb in her direction. "*Princess.*"

Evie grinned in spite of herself, then watched in disbelief as he hopped onto the counter and unscrewed the bottle. "That's some amazing self-control, peasant. You made it past dawn."

He rolled his eyes like she was being particularly dense.

"It's for my wounds, Highness."

She grinned again, but glanced back just a second later to see him taking a swig from the bottle. He froze when their eyes met, then continued drinking with a defensive shrug.

"...I'm hurting on the inside."

Asher left them to it, joining Freya at the counter.

"I can help," he offered, rolling up his sleeves. "If you just tell me what—"

"Oh, come on!" Evie interrupted with a laugh. "You're even worse than I am!"

"That's not possible," he replied stiffly. "I'm a natural born chef."

She perched on the counter opposite Seth, kicking her legs against the wood.

Vampires were notoriously convincing, and a less experienced person might have believed the indignation in those hypnotic eyes. But the princess had known Asher since he was five years old, sneaking into the nursery to file down his teeth in the dead of night.

It would take more than simple denial to throw her off his tracks.

"Your expertise extends so far as fetching water and burning raw meat over a fire. Anytime the three of us went camping, I always had to depend on Ellanden to make sure I wouldn't starve."

Seth lifted the bottle with a grin. "Because, heaven forbid, you learn to provide for yourself."

She leveled him with a cold glare. "*Princess*, remember?"

"That's absolutely absurd," Asher said with an air of authority, sprinkling an unnecessary handful of sugar into the bowl. "I'm perfectly capable of—"

"Why should you be?" Freya asked flatly, yanking the dish away. "It's not like you'll ever have a need for it."

The kitchen fell quiet as the others turned to look at her. Seth lowered the bottle slowly and Evie stared in amazement, wondering if the young witch had intended to be so sharp.

Asher stood there a moment then bowed his head, straightening the mess on the counter just to have something to do with his hands. "No, I suppose not—"

"In that case, do you mind giving me some room?" She elbowed past him, throwing a chunk of butter into the bowl. "Some of us are actually helping."

Yes...she definitely meant it.

The vampire froze where he stood, staring in surprise, then circled deliberately to the other side of the counter. After a few seconds of charged silence, he cleared his throat.

"You're angry with me?" he asked quietly.

She said nothing, merely pounded her fists into the dough.

Of all the young companions, the vampire and the witch were two of the least likely to have a confrontation. Not only did they get along splendidly but she still thought of him as a surrogate older brother, and he'd long ago been conditioned to navigate the most passionate of tempers. Never once had he found himself on the wrong side of that line. He wasn't quite sure how to get back.

After a few seconds of silence, he tried again.

"Because Ellanden and I got into a fight—"

"Why would I care that you and Ellanden got into a fight?" she fired back.

Evie glanced nervously between them, while Seth took another swig from the bottle. But Asher regarded her with that steady patience, the same way he had when she was just a girl.

"Freya...because Landi and I got into a fight?"

Sparks flew off her hands, shattering a nearby mug. The others jumped in surprise, bracing themselves as distant shouts echoed from down the hall, but the witch had gone very still.

She stared at the dough a moment, then lifted her head slowly.

"You pulled me back." Her lovely face was flushed with anger, but her voice was shockingly calm. "With the vampires. I was going to save him...and you pulled me back."

Seven hells.

Asher's lips parted in genuine surprise. Whatever he'd been expecting her to say, it most definitely hadn't been anything like that. "That's what you..."

A sudden chill fell over the kitchen as each one flashed back to the same memory: the young witch standing before the queen of the vampires, screaming her defiance, deadly lights rippling like hectic furies up and down her trembling arms.

"They were going to kill you," Asher said softly, staring deep into her eyes. "Freya...they were going to *kill* you. There was no way you could have—"

"You don't know that," she said stiffly, returning to her work. "You don't know what would have happened. At least I had the courage to fight. I didn't try to make deals with them, or give up at the slightest bit of resistance. And afterwards, I didn't act like everything was okay."

A charged silence fell over the kitchen, broken only by the occasional rise of angry voices as the fae battled each other at the other end of the hall.

"—*acting like a freaking child—*"

"—*strangle you with your bloody ponytail—*"

They were still frozen in place when the door swung open and Evianna swept inside in a tangle of frizzled hair and an unusual number of shawls. She took one look at the scene in front of her, lingering on the witch and the vampire, before glancing down at the countertop in delight.

"Oh, splendid—biscuits!"

<hr />

NEEDLESS TO SAY, IT wasn't a particularly great breakfast.

Freya was still fuming at Asher. Asher was still numb with shock. The fae were still locked in combat as one tried to sew the other's head. And Seth was drinking with the speed of someone accustomed only to direct physical violence, not the simmering emotional apprehension of a cold war.

Evie was trying to keep things together, but things were going from bad to worse.

"So...hyenas?" Evianna prompted cheerfully.

She alone was oblivious to the tension, happily shoveling biscuit after biscuit into her mouth as the others sat in charged silence, staring grimly at the center of the table.

"Yes—hyenas," Evie replied, grateful for the save. "At least we think they were hyenas. It was a little hard to tell. They swept down from the grasslands, caught us off guard—"

"Because no one was paying attention," Freya inserted coolly. "Because the vampire and the fae were busy beating each other to death at the edge of the forest." She took a huge biscuit for herself, flashing Evianna a sweet smile. "Like we don't have enough problems."

Seth raised the bottle, taking a long drink.

"So, uh...they caught us off guard," Evie continued uncertainly, feeling the hot prickle of nerves on the back of her neck. "It was touch and go, but we were able to fight them off."

A glass shattered in the bedroom, followed by a vengeful scream.

"Is that what broke the fae's head?" Evianna asked conversationally.

Okay, breakfast was a bad idea.

Four sets of eyes shot instinctively down the hallway, where the immortal battle was still underway, before returning awkwardly to the table.

"No," Seth muttered. "That was me."

"It *wasn't* you." Evie kicked his chair, forcing him to meet her eyes. "Even Landi doesn't blame you for that. It wasn't your fault—"

"If I had been paying attention—"

"Don't be ridiculous," Freya interrupted. "If you'd been paying attention? With the voices of thirty vampires rattling around in your head?" She turned with great authority to the witch, but every word she said was directed at Asher. "They forced a blood bond with him after wiping out a Kreo settlement. Dozens of them. He's been struggling just to stay sane."

Seth paled ever so slightly, tightening his grip on the bottle. "It isn't like that," he muttered. "It's not like I'm—"

"This one condones it," Freya continued angrily, jerking her head across the table. "He'd say anything to defend the vampires. He didn't even want to leave."

"That's enough," Evie chided her quietly. "The only reason we got out of there was because Asher offered to bond with the queen. He didn't want to stay. And for the record, Ellanden doesn't need you to fight his battles for him—"

"Ellanden is busy getting his head sewn back together, after what Asher would call an honest mistake," Freya shot back evenly. "And he *did* want to stay. Even if you don't want to admit it."

The girls glared at each other across the table. Seth was flat-out gulping the rum.

After a few drawn-out seconds, a quiet voice broke the silence.

"I don't condone anything that happened," Asher said softly. "What happened to the Kreo, what happened to Seth...I would give my life to change it." He paused a moment before looking Freya directly in the eyes. "But I also can't condone the murder of innocent—"

Freya threw back her head with a cold laugh.

"What—vampires?" she challenged. "*Innocent* vampires? Is there such a thing?"

There was a sharp scrape as Asher pushed back his chair, swiftly leaving the room. The others were still staring when Freya took off in the opposite direction, a butter knife clattering in her wake. The remaining women fell silent. Seth's fingers drummed nervously on the bottle.

Only then did Evie realize it was mostly empty. The shifter hadn't noticed yet himself. It wasn't until he lifted it to his mouth and missed that he abruptly realized he was drunk.

The princess watched with a secret smile as he glanced down in alarm then hurried to put it back in the cabinet, tripping slightly as he made his way past the chairs. He'd just made it back to the table, when the two fae appeared suddenly at the end of the hall—looking slightly worse for wear, but overall rather pleased with themselves. Their smiles froze as they surveyed the breakfast.

"What happened here?" Cosette asked in surprise.

Seth glanced around the table with a stricken expression.

"What, this?" he stammered. "Nothing. I mean, nothing to worry about. Just some short tempers. Not a big deal. Except for the end. And how it started, and that bit in the middle. *I'd* never seen anything like it before. But the Red Hand wasn't big on family breakfast, so I guess..." He trailed off, realizing that he'd been talking for quite a while. "...I wouldn't really know."

APPROVAL 33

Cosette's eyebrows rose slowly. And Ellanden forgot his pre-rehearsed speech about the perils of cross-stitch and regarded the shifter with a slight grin.

"What's the matter with you? Why are you talking like that?"

"Like what?"

Seth leaned casually against the wall, then his elbow slipped.

"Are you drunk?" Ellanden asked in surprise.

The shifter scoffed like it was ridiculous, but avoided meeting his eyes. "That's an interesting question," he answered, backing casually toward the door. "I'm going to check on the boat. See if there's a way to salvage it..."

"Can you manage the ladder?" Evie called innocently.

He shot her a quick look, then vanished outside.

Three down, three to go...

The fae stared after him before turning back to the table.

All that remained amongst the abandoned place-settings was a stricken princess and a gluttonous witch—still happily scarfing down whatever was left of the biscuits.

There was a chance she hadn't noticed the others had gone.

"...what did we miss?"

THE REST OF THE DAY was spent in seclusion.

There weren't many places one could seek privacy in a swamp, but the friends still managed to spread out until none of them was in direct contact with any other. Half were afraid they'd start fighting, half were afraid they wouldn't be able to stop.

If they were at all worried this might offend their strange hostess, those fears were quickly laid to rest. Evianna seemed just as content without them as she was in their company. More than anything, she seemed content to wait. As if nothing they did could surprise her. As if every strained argument and adolescent rebellion was par for the course.

It wasn't until the sun went down and Evie wandered back to the house that she realized the others were already inside. No one was talking, but no one had gone to their rooms either. Everyone was gathered in the living room, sitting in silence in front of a large fire.

Evianna flashed a smile as she entered, tilting her head towards a steaming pot of tea.

The princess drifted automatically towards the kitchen for a mug—feeling strangely at home, considering the circumstances, but stopped suddenly in front of a painting on the wall.

It was slightly smaller than the rest—a beautiful landscape with a flock of white birds soaring serenely across the sky. But it wasn't the majesty of the picture or the delicacy of the brushstrokes that caught the princess' attention. It was the strange feeling she'd seen a picture like it before.

Michael.

She stepped closer, resting her fingers lightly upon the frame.

"How long have you known them?" she asked suddenly, glancing over her shoulder towards the living room. "Michael and Petra."

The others looked up in surprise, but Evianna only smiled—glancing fondly at the painting before gesturing the young princess to sit by the fire.

"I met Petra and Michael when they were just teenagers—no older than you. They were chasing some wretched beast through the mountains. Five weeks hunting, they were still on its trail."

The day's private dilemmas fell away as the friends straightened up with interest. It was hard to imagine the famed siblings ever being teenagers. At some point or another, each of the friends had come to the independent decision that they'd never been young. Not ever.

"A beast?" Ellanden repeated, eyes dancing in the firelight. Stories such as these had always been his favorite. "What kind of beast?"

Evianna kicked back in her chair with a chuckle.

"Who can remember? The world wasn't the same then as it is now. The realm was crawling with the filthy creatures. At any rate, they were having a bit of trouble. When I wandered into the woods and found them, both had lost their weapons in the grass. When the beast reared up to finish them off, I took matters into my own hands."

She took a long drink of tea, staring into the fire with a faint smile. As if the story was over. As if the friends weren't hanging on her every word.

"Took matters into your own hands?" Evie finally repeated, perched on the very edge of her seat. "What happened?"

The witch glanced up in surprise.

"Oh—I turned it into a guinea fowl. We roasted it over the fire."

There was a beat of silence.

Then the friends burst out laughing.

This part was far easier to imagine. Their adoptive grandparents were nothing if not practical. Once the beast lost the ability to destroy entire villages, it promptly qualified as lunch.

"They came to me, you know," Evianna continued suddenly. "Brought me to the palace a decade past. I didn't want to go. Not only are royal parties tiresome affairs, but that's not the way these things happen. I'm not meant to track down subjects of divine intervention; they're supposed to come to me. In their own time, in their own way."

A shiver ran up Evie's arms as she remembered Michael's words outside Harenthall, when he'd rescued them from the library's deadly fall.

'Maybe if I hadn't interfered, the fates would have revealed some new path for you. Maybe the fall from the window would have...'

He'd never finished that sentence, but the princess knew exactly what he was going to say. If he hadn't caught them that day, swooping down on the wings of an eagle, maybe she would have found wings of her own. Maybe if he hadn't done it himself, the dragon inside would finally fly.

Evianna clapped her hands briskly. "Anyway, they convinced me, we set up that ridiculous carnival tent, and the rest is history."

A succinct summary. It just left one or two things out.

"It isn't history at all," Ellanden murmured. "We're right in the middle of it." He stood up suddenly, pacing in front of the hearth. "I'll be honest, I didn't want to come here last night because I thought there was a decent chance you might roast *us* over the fire. But in all seriousness, we can't stay. If you don't know the reason for this encounter any more than we do ourselves, we must be moving on. We've lost too much time already—"

The witch threw back her head with a raspy chuckle, freezing him in his tracks. "Sometimes I forget, you're only half Fae." She stared at him affectionately, eyes dancing in the light of the fire. "Those years spent in the wizard's cave. You consider that lost time, do you?"

The prince lifted his chin, answering a bit sharply, "Considering I spent most of it sleeping on the floor of a cage while a deranged sorcerer drained years of my life away—*yes*, I consider it lost."

A valid point. But the witch simply shook her head.

"There is no such thing as *lost* time. You were overeager. Perhaps Michael and Petra were overeager as well. They wanted to prevent things. To *preempt* things. But that isn't the way prophecy works. The realm was not yet ready. The darkness had not yet spread. And all those people whose hearts you'll need to sway had not those ten years of suffering to prepare them."

An abrupt silence fell over the room as the friends stared at the woman in shock.

Everything about her was startling. From her laughter, to her appearance, to her comatose sleep patterns, to the sudden bursts of invaluable wisdom she doled out in front of the fire.

Was this really the same woman who'd tricked them into making her breakfast? Could she really be right about the prophecy? Had the world simply needed more time?

"So...this is really *your* fault," Freya said wisely.

There was a beat of silence, then the witch burst out laughing again.

"Yes, my dear—if that makes things easier. It was my fault. The next time I receive a message from the heavens, I'll be sure to keep it to myself."

Even the friends were forced to laugh at that, though they were all feeling unexpectedly thoughtful— gazing pensively into the fire.

"At any rate, there's no need to hurry on with your quest," the witch concluded. "Time moves differently here. And while I may have been surprised at your arrival, the reason for it is quickly becoming clear."

Her eyes drifted from one to another, seeing things the others couldn't. Bruises that had already faded. Wounds that were no longer there.

"And what is that?" Asher asked softly.

Evianna looked up suddenly, as if she'd been roused from a dream. "We've spoken enough. It's time for all of you to rest."

The princess opened her mouth to protest, but no sooner had the witch said the words than she was struck with an overwhelming feeling of fatigue. It hadn't come on suddenly, she realized, but had been building for a very long time. Always repressed in the heat of the moment. Always put off until some distant future in which they might have more time.

Without saying a word the friends rose from their chairs and drifted down the hallway, murmuring words of goodnight as they split off to their separate rooms. Evie stood up slowly, the last to leave. She stared after them a moment before turning back to the witch.

"You say Michael and Petra convinced you...*how* did they convince you?"

The witch's eyes twinkled as she smoothed a lock of the princess' fiery hair. "They told me in no uncertain terms that you were touched by destiny. They told me in all their years, in all their travels...such a thing had never been so clearly written in the stars." She flicked her fingers, extinguishing the fire. "Now get some rest, my darling. You need to catch your breath."

Chapter 4

The princess didn't sleep much that night. Exhausted, and yet unable to rest. She spent the hours staring at the ceiling instead, watching the moonlit shadows, replaying those final words in her mind.

'They told me in no uncertain terms that you were touched by destiny. They told me in all their years, in all their travels…such a thing had never been so clearly written in the stars.'

When at last the sun broke through the trees she arose with a new mantra, determined to live up to her grandparents' convictions. Determined to make them her own.

Whatever it takes.

With almost comical haste she jumped out of bed and raced across the room, only to glance down and find a small bundle of fabric on the floor. She picked it up slowly, rubbing it between her fingers, then lifted it higher as a lovely dress tumbled to the ground.

Her lips parted in surprise.

When the friends had first arrived, they were cold and hungry. Many were still wearing the clothes they'd donned for the Kreo feast. Many had forgotten the feel of an actual bed.

It seemed the witch had taken each as a personal challenge.

A tiny smile crept up her face as she discarded what she was wearing and slipped the gown over her head. It was light as a feather. Fitted on top, but free on the bottom—cascading to the tips of her toes in delicate shades of blue. She smoothed the skirt and moved to the window for a look, staring at her reflection in the glass. The bruises were almost healed. Her hair was long and messy.

With quick hands she braided the strands that framed her face and pulled them back in a twisted knot, leaving the rest to tumble down between her shoulder blades. A few stubborn tendrils refused to conform, falling free from the rest and brushing gently against her cheeks.

Too simple for a princess. Too pretty for a weather-hardened traveler. But somehow, given the fresh resolve of the morning, it seemed exactly right.

She yanked open the door and rushed down the hall as fast as her feet would carry her. A part of her was tempted to find Evianna, to thank her immediately for the gown, but there were urgent matters to deal with first. The witch had told them last night that the reason for their visit was becoming increasingly clear. After the disastrous breakfast attempt and the hours of isolation that had followed, the princess was beginning to see that reason for herself.

They were fighting an unknown enemy over a missing stone, in a forgotten wasteland, and the fate of the realm was at stake. They could not afford to be divided. It was time to come together.

And I know exactly where to start...

THE FUNNY THING ABOUT having revelatory moments with one's best friends was that it often gave them the same ideas. Most of the others were already gone by the time Evie got up, wandering along the river in their own existential angst or staring fixedly at the horizon, building up resolve.

The Prince of the Fae was doing a little of both.

"Ellanden?" she called softly as she headed towards him, picking her way carefully across the soggy shoreline to stand by his side. "What are you doing out here?"

He glanced over briefly, then returned his eyes to the sky. "Contemplating flight."

She fought back a smile, nodding seriously instead. Of all her charismatic friends, the fae was only ever half-joking when he said such a thing. Not only was he prone to dangerous fits of whimsy, but the ability to manifest angelic wings and take to the sky actually ran in his family.

"Think you could carry me, too?" she asked lightly.

He laughed to himself, eyeing the clouds. "When have I ever *not* carried you?"

They stood there a while, following the progress of a pair of birds as they made their way in a slow arc across the sky. Twisting and looping together before vanishing beyond the horizon.

He continued to search. She cast him a shy glance.

"How are you?"

It was a delicate question, deceptively casual, while implying a whole lot more. The kind that was usually dismissed with a roll of the eyes. But the fae didn't respond how she'd expect.

"I'm...unsteady."

She glanced at him in surprise, making a quick study of his face in profile before looking back to the sky. The birds had disappeared. She'd already forgotten what they looked like.

"I can understand that," she said softly, venturing farther and farther onto thin ice. "We've started to almost...almost *dismiss* these things, but Ellanden, we honestly thought you'd died—"

"Not like that," he said sharply. Sharper than he'd intended. He tempered it with a quick sideways smile, noticing the dress for the first time. "My head feels fine."

She seized the smile like a life raft, determined to coax another. "Thanks to Cosette..."

He laughed suddenly, glancing back towards the house.

"In spite of her best efforts, I'm going to live." He winced at the memory before glancing again at the princess. "Seriously, Evie, we've given her far too much leeway. And a thousand curses on the person who thought it wise to teach her how to use a blade."

...that was probably you.

They stared at the water a while longer, watching abnormally-sized frogs jump in and out of the pond. It was warm. The kind of moist, clingy warmth that made the princess wonder if it would ever be cool. A gust of sticky air blew into her face, rattling the delicate braids.

"Landi," she began slowly, hesitant to break that fragile calm, "what was the question you wanted answered? When you went on a vision quest of your own?"

Another dangerous question, one to which she almost didn't expect an answer. Spontaneous personal queries rarely went over well, especially about his less-favored heritage. But the fae pulled in a deep breath, staring with an unexpectedly thoughtful expression at the cresting waves.

"I wanted to know if I should stay and be trained as a priest," he finally answered, those dark eyes fixed upon the water. "Or if I should return to Taviel."

The princess nodded automatically, then froze dead still.

"...*what?!*"

He sighed under his breath, raking back his tangled hair. "Be quiet, Everly."

"Are you *serious*?!" she exclaimed, making no effort whatsoever to check herself. "You *actually* asked if—"

He clapped a hand over her mouth. "Lower your voice, or I'll drown you in the lake."

She peeled off his fingers, still reeling. "I'm sorry, I just...I can't believe you would ever consider that."

No sooner would the sun reverse its orbit. No sooner would the stars fall out of the sky.

Ask any fae about their homeland, and they'd answer the same way. Taviel was more than just a city. It was an idea, a challenge, a promise fulfilled. The ivory streets and gleaming citadel were imprinted in the very heart of its people, a beacon of hope to every new generation.

APPROVAL 43

Hundreds of years they'd wandered the earth, but they always came back to the same place to lay their heads.

And Ellanden was their prince. The *prince* of all that.

A hundred questions formed on the tip of her tongue, but she abruptly realized none of them mattered. Whatever the fever dream had told him, a decision had been made. He had come back. The logistics, the timeline, none of the rest of it mattered. In the end, only a single question remained.

"...why?"

He gave a short laugh, staring at the murky water. "Why would I prefer Taviel to whatever primal sand pit the Kreo had chosen to pitch their tents?" he quipped. "I know it's been ten years, but have you already forgotten the Ivory City?"

Each word stung like a slap to the face. He'd always been good at that. Warm and smiling and inviting...until the precise moment he was not. Careful lines had been drawn around anything of value, and only he knew exactly where they were. Most people would retreat to a safer distance.

The princess shook her head.

"I don't buy that," she said quietly. "I can't believe you'd reject it purely on aesthetics. And that primal sand pit has a hold on you, whether you like it or not."

She remembered the look on his face when they'd first seen the Kreo settlement, the familial attachment that warmed his eyes. She remembered the way he'd mouthed the words to the blessing, the way his lips softened with a wistful smile as he watched the villagers dancing around the fire.

"People have always liked that about you," he murmured, eyes on the swamp. "You see past deflection, cut to the center—never afraid to speak your mind."

Those enchanting eyes shot to her face.

"I *dislike* those things."

They stared at each other for a long moment then laughed quietly, letting things fall back into place. He was good at that, too. Disarmament. It was something they'd learned from each other.

"The Kreo are impressive," she said leadingly, flicking the toe of her boot in the water. A crescent of tiny ripples eased away from the shore. "You must admit that. Even the young ones—"

"Not impressive enough, apparently."

She flashed a sideways glance, but moved on.

"Your mom always made it sound like something sacred. Like they were all teachers. Trusted to pass magic on to the next generation..."

She trailed off when a shadow flickered in his eyes.

"Magic," she repeated, watching him closely. Yes, this was definitely the trigger. "But how could you oppose that? The Fae are magic as well—"

"It's not the same thing."

For the first time, she could tell he was actually angry. The rest had been theater, to throw people off course. He sucked in a quick breath, frustrated with himself for speaking, then stared out at the water with the same expression as when she'd first walked outside.

"Magic," he murmured, like a gentle curse. "My entire life...upended by magic."

The princess stared back apprehensively, not knowing what to say. But the prince didn't need her to say anything. He'd been saying it to himself since long before dawn.

"Ten years we were trapped in enchanted slumber as a psychotic man in a cave drained our life away...magic did that. Freya was raised in horror by a woman hell-bent on using her power for herself. Magic did that. The spell that possessed Uncle Kailas, the trick rope designed to keep Seth enslaved." He spoke with quiet intensity, picking up speed as he gestured around the swamp. "Why are we even here—chasing down a magical stone before it can be used to destroy everything we see around us? Every bit of light and happiness. All the people we hold dear."

His eyes tightened and he looked away.

"All the darkness in this world...magic is to blame."

Evie pulled in a breath but found herself on uneven ground. Hopelessness wasn't a state they often entertained, and the fae wasn't generally bitter. It had taken a lot to make him say these things now. That being said, nothing he claimed was technically untrue.

It was quiet long enough that he was about to go back inside, then she caught his sleeve.

"Magic didn't do that," she said softly. "Magic didn't create the darkness. People did that. If they didn't have magic, they'd do it all the same."

His lips thinned in a hard smile. "But with what degree of success?"

She ignored this, staring deep into his eyes. "Magic brought our family together."

"*Tragedy* brought our family together," he corrected sharply. "They fought their way through it. They've been fighting ever since."

This from a boy who'd nailed pictures of fictional monsters to his wall. The same boy who'd refused to remove his cape for a year of childhood, chattering constantly about heroes and fate.

The same boy who'd been held captive ten years in a cave.

"You know that isn't true," she countered, standing between him and the house. "From the second my mother slipped that stone into the crown, she effectively safeguarded the entire realm."

He nodded quietly, but his eyes were unbearably sad.

"And now another stone can destroy it."

...yes.

It was true. Everything he said was true. That was the problem in arguing with a fae. They had this infuriating tendency to make sense. The years of suffering, the things they'd sacrificed, the people who had died...everything he said was true. There was just one problem.

It didn't matter.

It's the world we inherited. It's the prophecy we wanted. It's the commitment we made.

She saw her own reflection in those eternal eyes.

"That's where we come in."

She thought he was going to walk away, but he didn't. She thought he was going to yell or curse or maybe drown her in the lake after all, but he didn't. He just smiled—a beautiful, hopeful, unlikely smile that seemed to surprise him just as much as it did herself. After a few seconds of silence he nodded quietly, eyes twinkling as he glanced down and gave her dress a quick tug.

"Looks like you're getting ready to leave."

She laughed quietly, smoothing down the folds. "As fate would have it—I am. Care to join me?"

His eyes danced in the early morning light. "...when have I ever *not* joined you?"

One down...four to go.

They were still staring at each other, lost in the moment, when there was a murderous cry on the other side of the shore. The bushes rattled violently, throttled at the very roots, then a blurry figure emerged. Freya tumbled after it with a shriek, throwing herself headfirst into the swamp.

They looked over slowly, blinking in silence as she thrashed and flailed.

"What...is happening?"

Evie shook her head faintly, squinting for a better look. "I don't know."

In a flash they left their spot on the beach behind and raced along the uneven bank, making it to the witch just a half-second behind Asher—who'd heard her scream.

"What are you doing?!" he exclaimed, staring incredulously at the bog.

She was up to her chin in the water, but she didn't appear to be in trouble. Rather, she was making trouble for something else. A stream of bubbles was rising to the surface from somewhere beneath her, but every time it tried to make an appearance she squashed it back down.

"Mending fences."

He shook his head slowly as the others slid to a stop beside him, staring with matching expressions as the witch thrashed back and forth in a chaotic flailing of limbs.

"Should we..." Seth hesitated, unsure how to finish the sentence. "I don't know...should we try to get her out of there?"

Evie raised her eyebrows, weighing their chances.

Even if they'd wanted to, it didn't seem likely. Whatever the young witch was trying to do she was fully committed, letting out preemptive shrieks of triumph before hurling her body beneath the surface. Flashes of light exploded in the water, followed by an unearthly cry.

Ellanden stared a second longer before nudging Evie forward.

"Do something," he muttered under his breath.

"Me?" Evie cried, side-stepping a splash of putrid water. "Why me? Cosette's her friend."

Cosette shook her head. "...not today."

"You're crazy," Evie said practically. "And she's clearly gone crazy, too." She shot him a withering look as Freya piped up from the bog.

"I'm not crazy!" she panted, kicking at something below the waves. "I'm...*working*!"

With a savage cry she vanished beneath the water.

The others stared for a moment, then continued talking.

"Besides, you're on this big reunification kick," Ellanden continued, stepping aside quickly so a splash of water hit Seth in the face. "This should be right up your alley."

The princess shot him a disbelieving glare, and he rolled his eyes.

"Oh, come on...you come swooping down from the house, beaming at the horizon, asking insufferably personal questions, wearing a brand new dress. There may as well have been orchestral swells behind you. Ten gold coins said you actually heard them."

...we've got to stop spending so much time together.

"What are you talking about?" Seth asked curiously.

"Nothing," they shot back in unison.

Another rabid cry tore from the water, and Ellanden turned to the vampire instead.

"Ash—get her out of there before she drowns."

Before she drowns something else.

Asher cast him a stricken look but the others had all taken a uniform step backwards, leaving him standing closest to the water. He registered it a moment too late.

"Don't do that," he complained. "I *hate* it when you do that!"

Ellanden smirked, while Evie pointed with theatric fright.

"Quick—save the witch!"

He steeled himself up with another sigh before taking a step towards the water—stopping just short of the phosphorescent waves. The witch was only half-visible, vanishing for seconds on end before suddenly reappearing in a spray of slime. He cleared his throat—giving it his best shot.

"...Freya?"

Splash.

"...could you come out of there?"

She resurfaced in a grotesque coating of green, clutching at something beneath her.

"Not yet!" she cried with eyes closed. "I'm doing something important!"

Asher opened his mouth, then paused. "I can never tell if she's being serious—"

"She is," Cosette interrupted wearily. "She *is* being serious."

There was another mighty splash, but this one was followed by a genuine scream.

"Freya!"

Without a second thought Asher dove into the water after her, vanishing until a thin stream of bubbles rose to the surface. At this point the others stopped their teasing and tensed at the same time, watching to see what would happen. It was quiet for a few seconds. A few seconds longer than any of them would have liked. Then the vampire surfaced with a gasp, holding the witch in his arms.

She had something in her arms as well.

"What is that?" Evie asked in astonishment as he dragged them both to shore.

It looked like a small beaver. Large teeth, matted fur, but with a thin, rat-like tail. Little tufts of human hair were wedged beneath its claws, and the corners of its mouth were bloody.

It was also undisputedly dead.

The pair collapsed in the mud, panting with exhaustion, putrid water streaming off their clothes. Asher rolled onto his back, holding his face in both hands, while Freya took a second to recover then smashed the bloody carcass onto his chest.

"Here...it's for you."

His eyes shot open in alarm and he sat up slowly, staring as though she'd gone mad. The body inched down the front of his shirt, leaving a trail of viscera and blood behind it.

Seth began shaking with silent laughter. Ellanden lifted a hand to his mouth.

"What..." Asher trailed off with a grimace, sucking in a sharp breath and turning stiffly so the thing plopped back onto the mud. "Why would you—"

"It's my apology for the other day," she panted, still trying to catch her breath. When she saw his bewildered stare, she gestured to the creature. "Lots of blood in those things."

Lots of...?

It took a second to register. Then all at once the friends understood.

Apparently, the princess wasn't the only one trying to stitch things back together and make amends. Since yesterday's biscuits had been a disaster, the witch was determined to set things right.

Asher was the last to connect the dots, quite possibly because he'd swallowed a great deal of swamp water and both ears were still ringing. His eyes travelled twice between the repulsive carcass and the witch's beaming smile before lifting tentatively to her face.

"...you made me breakfast?"

She collapsed into the mud. "I made you breakfast."

Chapter 5

'The day the witch made the vampire breakfast' would live in infamy, but at the moment all Asher would say was that he needed a bath. His girlfriend waited dutifully for him in the bedroom, silently mouthing all the jokes she *wanted* to make, so by the time he returned she'd be solemn and supportive. That strategy lasted all of four seconds.

"You get those intestines out of your hair?"

He froze halfway through the door, looking up in surprise. For a few seconds the two of them just stared at each other, then he bowed his head with a sigh.

"Go on—let's hear them."

"*The forest animals called, they want their friend back.*"

"*They say breakfast is the most important meal of the day.*"

"*Now you can have an undead pet!*"

"*What did the witch give to the vampire?*"

He held up his hand.

"All right, that enough—"

"*Rabies.*"

He pursed his lips, staring in silence. "...are you finished?"

"Yes." She nodded with great satisfaction, patting the mattress beside her. "Jokes aside, Ash, I really hope you didn't eat that thing. By the look of it, that wasn't the first time it died in a swamp."

He shook his head, wet hair dripping onto his shoulders. "After what it went through, I gave it a proper burial."

A new voice echoed from the hall. "I have a terrible feeling you're going to say that about me one day..."

The couple looked up to see Ellanden in the doorway. He flashed a quick smile then slipped inside, standing rather awkwardly with his hands in his pockets, eyes fixed on the floor.

After a few awkward seconds, he cleared his throat.

"I came to let you apologize."

So. Typical. Ellanden.

The princess' eyes snapped shut in exasperation, but the vampire regarded him with the hint of a smile. "You came to let me apologize?" he repeated. "That's very gracious of you."

The fae nodded distractedly. "Well, everyone else seems to be scrambling for an olive branch, and since I'm fresh out of corpses to throw at you, I figured giving you the chance to absolve yourself was the next best thing."

There was an excruciating pause.

"...since *I'm* the one who needs to apologize?"

"That's right."

A rather bold assumption, especially considering vampire was still sporting almost every wound from their skirmish before the hyena attack. In contrast, after getting his head sewn back together like a particularly obstinate doll, the Prince of the Fae was actually looking much better.

It was a predicament both men seemed to realize at the same time.

The vampire glanced at the cuts on his hands. The fae handled it with his customary grace.

"I don't think those were from me," he said evasively, unwilling to look at it straight on. "You probably just tripped over something. Or maybe you got a splinter from the boat—"

"Evie," Asher interrupted quietly, "why don't you wait outside?"

She shook her head slowly, curling up on the bed. "Oh, no...I want to see this."

The fae ignored her completely, sweeping inside and slamming the door.

"What did you expect?" he snapped. "You come at me with fangs bared—"

"I know."

"Seth was a wreck—"

"I know."

"And there I am, trying to comfort the poor boy—"

"I know."

"Stop arguing and listen!" Ellanden pulled him to his feet, giving his collar an automatic straightening before shoving him into the wall. "You made it sound as though he was being impolite! As if the world should simply allow for the homicidal nature of those who would wish him harm!"

The vampire nodded silently, eyes on the floor.

"They *forced* a blood bond. In what world could you possibly defend such a thing? In what world could it come between us? An *eternal bond* he'll be forced to carry the rest of his life!"

"Yes," Asher said quietly.

"And when I tried to—" Ellanden paused, coming up short. "...yes?"

"Yes."

"I don't understand."

"I'm agreeing with you. You're right."

There was a long pause.

"Did someone just teach you that?" Ellanden finally asked, playing the exchange back in his mind. "*You're right.* I've never heard you use that phrase—"

"Cio," Asher interrupted quietly. "All my life, we've been family. There is not a thing in this world that could come between us. Do I really need to tell you why?"

Their eyes met and both men warmed with the same smile.

"...*kiss.*"

The moment shattered as they turned in astonishment to the girl on the bed.

"What?!"

"What?!"

"Just a little," Evie prompted. "Just this once—"

Asher shoved her off the bed.

"Hilarious," he muttered under his breath.

Ellanden waited until she was standing, then shoved her down again.

"Everyone's gathering outside to see if we can repair the boat." He cocked his head towards the hallway. "You coming?"

"Absolutely."

Asher grabbed his coat and headed to the door.

"Oh," the fae remembered suddenly, "I came up with a few jokes about—"

"Keep walking."

The princess pulled herself up slowly, rubbing at the bruises on her arm. Jokes aside, it had been the confrontation she'd been fearing most. The one that had been building since long before they stepped into that cave. There was only one other that could match it.

"Ellanden." She made it to the door just as Seth stepped out of his room, catching the fae by the arm. "Can I speak with you a moment?"

The two men lingered awkwardly in the hallway as Asher shrugged and headed outside to meet the rest of them. Evie melted back into her bedroom, watching through a crack in the door.

It was quiet for a few seconds as the shifter braced himself to speak.

"I don't know how to thank you," he finally managed. "For what you did."

The memory came back in a rush, just a bunch of splinters.

The boulder creaking loose, the fae sprinting towards him. The sharp impact around his ribs as he went flying to safety. The quieter *crack* as the prince went sprawling across the grass.

APPROVAL

The images haunted him. Not for a single moment had they left his mind.

But the shifter wasn't the only one struggling. Ellanden went from surprised, to wary, to so *extremely* wary it came off as flippant and rude.

"Don't be ridiculous," he said stiffly. "You would have done the same."

He turned without another word, the encounter already stretching well past his limit, but in a move so casual it was almost by accident Seth eased smoothly in front of him.

"I don't know if that's true," he confessed with a little grin. "I'd like to think so, but if we're being honest...you're kind of a bastard."

Ellanden stared in astonishment as the princess fought back a smile.

Silence filled the hall for a few seconds, then the fae laughed in spite of himself. The tension lifted as he nodded at nothing in particular, raking his fingers back through his hair. "Yeah, well...you make it easy."

They shared a grin, lingering inadvertently in the hall.

"When you pushed me towards those hungry vampires," the fae continued, "volunteered to leave me behind as a sacrifice, that was a particularly nice touch."

Seth nodded with a thoughtful frown. "That was *after* you tried to leave me in the arena. Or was it *before*? I can never remember."

They laughed again, but Ellanden's smile faded as he looked into the shifter's eyes. Just a few seconds and there wasn't a trace. It was replaced with something harder to understand.

"I wasn't trying to appease you, back in the forest," he said suddenly. "I wasn't just trying to make you stay. You're a part of this group now. We protect each other."

His eyes softened as they found the fading marks on the shifter's body.

"I should be thanking you," Ellanden murmured. His eyes flitted down the hall, almost like he could see Cosette on the other side. "She means everything to me. You kept her alive."

It should have been a touching moment, but neither man looked particularly moved. Instead they were appraising. As if poised on the edge of something that might finally move.

"But you don't want us together."

Seth's voice was flat and hard, already anticipating the answer, already resenting the fact that the opinion of another would most assuredly sway the decision of the girl he'd decided to love.

Ellanden stared another moment, surprised he'd be so direct.

Then he shook his head.

"No, I don't."

❦

THE BOAT WAS WRECKED, there was no salvaging it. The friends stood around it uselessly for a few minutes, feeling all their forward momentum shift on a dime. It wasn't until Freya offered to find another handful of rodents they might paddle downstream that they dispersed with muted laughter and headed back inside.

Lunch was waiting. A kind of lopsided stew. Dinner was not long after that.

Evianna hadn't been lying. Time did move at a difference pace in her little pocket of the world.

No sooner had the friends finished at the table than they realized the sun had already set, and it wasn't long until they'd be going to bed. They washed quickly, keeping interactions to a minimum, but found themselves forsaking their previous sleeping arrangements and gathering together in a single room.

"We're going to regret this," Freya declared, stretching out on the mattress. "The second we're back in the real world, we're going to regret not using the extra beds."

"What do you care?" Seth teased, tugging her hair from the floor below. "Since you already claimed this one for yourself—"

"I thought we agreed that was fair," the witch interrupted quickly, sensing that a discussion might not go her way. "Since I almost drowned this morning making sure Asher didn't starve, it makes sense that I'd get the bed."

Asher shook his head with a faint smile, propped up beside the window. "What a fascinating interpretation..."

Evie took his hand with a smile, resting her head on his shoulder.

It was strange. They'd only been in the little cabin for two nights—two nights of stress and nightmares and bickering—yet she felt completely different than when they'd first arrived.

Perhaps the witch was right. They'd only needed a moment to catch their breath.

"I wonder what she meant about time," Cosette murmured. She was lying on the window sill above Asher, her long hair trailing down to touch the top of his head. "That it moves differently over here." Her dark eyes flashed up to the others. "Do you think that means nothing will have changed? That we'll pick up exactly where we left off?"

"You're assuming we'll get back," Ellanden answered, staring off into the night. "Unless we start walking and hope the enchantment wears off, we still have to figure that part out."

The others fell silent, all thinking the same thing.

They had decided to leave in the morning. Standing over the broken body of their boat, it was the only thing they'd decided for sure. Granted, none of them had any idea exactly how.

I'm sure our hostess could give us a friendly nudge...

The princess pushed suddenly to her feet, picking her way across the room.

"I'm going to speak with Evianna. Try to get some sleep." Her eyes rested a moment on each one, waiting until they met her eyes. "We'll be leaving in the morning."

She was met with a spattering of smiles, a chorus of goodnights, and one highly-sarcastic salute which she decided to cherish most of all. The others settled down for the evening, blowing out the candles, lying down to sleep. The last light had just been extinguished, when she paused suddenly at the door, glancing back towards the window.

"Cosette?" she called softly, waiting until the girl lifted her head. "What did you mean when you said that this place is cloaked?"

The fae exchanged a quick look with Freya.

"Some enchantments are so powerful, they can prevent a place from being seen. Whether by intention, or even stumbled upon by accident. If those residing inside don't want to be found, then they won't." She paused, continuing almost painfully, "It's the same spell our parents are using."

The conversation jerked to a halt, like all the air had been sucked from the room. A silence fell over them, so harsh and raw that the lovely fae was overcome with the need to break it.

"You were dead," she said quietly. "It wasn't a question. Everyone knew you were dead."

There was another pause.

"A part of them died, too."

⁂

EVIANNA WAS LYING IN her favorite recliner when the princess answered, holding one glass of liquor and offering out another as if she'd expected the company. Evie stood there for a moment, considering, then walked back to Michael's portrait instead.

"Can I ask you a question?"

The old woman smiled. "Seems to be."

Evie glanced over her shoulder.

"Will you answer it directly?"

Every screaming instinct told her no. Every chipped teacup and steamed window and wilted flower in the enchanted house told her no.

To be contrary, the witch shrugged with a smile. "Maybe," she taunted.

Evie's eyes drifted back to the paint. "Do you know which of us is going to die?"

Her spine stiffened as she said it, and she listened very closely—hoping the woman might do something to give herself away. When listening became too much she turned suddenly, staring right into the witch's eyes. They were surprised. She hadn't expected that.

"Which of you will die?" Evianna repeated faintly.

The princess drew a sharp breath, quoting the woman's own words.

"Three shall set out, though three shall not return..." She paused a moment, letting them sink in. "Will it be just one of us? All of us? Do you already know?"

The witch stared another moment, wide eyes reflecting the glow of the dying fire, then she shook her head with a sad smile. "These things always tend to fall upon such young people," she murmured almost to herself. "I've always wondered why that is."

Evie stood there in silence, caught off guard.

"Why does that matter?" she finally asked.

The witch glanced up suddenly, like she'd forgotten anyone else was there. Her eyes crinkled with a faint smile as she rattled the ice in her glass.

"It's because you have hope," she answered her own question. "Hope is the thing that drives us. Even when it's impossible, even when it's threatened. Young people have that in spades."

She doesn't know. Or she won't tell me.

She turned back to the painting.

That probably means it's me.

"Did my parents have it?"

She didn't mean to ask. She didn't even know she was thinking it until the words tumbled out of her mouth. She turned around slowly, wishing she'd taken that drink.

"They've locked themselves away, did you know that?" she asked softly. "Far from the rest of the world, where no one will ever find them. Doesn't sound like hope to me."

Evianna set down her glass, looking at her thoughtfully. "You think there's been a mistake?" she asked. "A miscalculation of some kind?"

Sudden tears pricked the princess' eyes and she looked away quickly. For the hundredth time, Michael's words floating through her mind.

Maybe if I hadn't interfered, the fates would have revealed some new path for you...

"My darling girl, you were always meant to try!" The chair scraped behind her as the old witch pushed to her feet with an affectionate chuckle. "Neither your parents, nor your kingdoms, nor anyone in the realm ever stood a chance of stopping you. The fates might work in mysterious ways, but you were chosen for a reason. Always remember that."

Evie tried to smile, but it fell flat.

"But you don't really know that, do you?" she asked quietly. "You weren't even supposed to be at the castle that night. Maybe someone else would have done better. Maybe one of the boys—"

"I appeared to the boys, but they didn't see me."

The princess stopped cold, her mouth falling open in shock. "...you did?"

Evianna nodded slowly, deep lines creasing around her eyes. "I set up the tent, called out to them—they walked right past me as if I wasn't even there. It wasn't until you wandered down the lawn that it was clear I was always meant to have come."

A sudden burst of relief warmed the princess from head to toe. But no sooner had she registered it than her heart chilled with a stab of dread.

"So then it's me?" she whispered. "I'm the one who's going to die?"

Evianna took a step back, looked at her shrewdly.

"Would that make a difference?" she finally asked. "Would it make you turn back?"

The two women locked eyes.

"No."

Evianna stared a moment longer, then stepped forward with a twinkling smile. "In that case don't worry about the fates, little princess." She wrapped a wiry arm around her and led her back down the hall. "I have a feeling they have great things in store for you..."

Chapter 6

"I don't understand...a portal?"

The six friends stood on one side of the porch while Evianna stood on the other. She'd made them wait a bit for her answer, probably just to score another free meal, but now that the breakfast dishes were cleaned and put away she finally seemed ready to help them.

"Yes, my darling." She stepped forward without thinking, running a hand along the side of Seth's face. "So handsome," she murmured. "It's always the shifters that get me."

He raised his eyebrows and vowed not to ask any more questions, while Evie stepped between them with a frown. "But you're serious?" she pressed. "You can make a portal?"

It was hard to keep the note of accusation from her voice. All the more so because, instead of looking remotely abashed, the woman simply gave them a toothy smile.

"Can I make a portal—HA!" She let loose a spray of spit, and they took a collective step backwards. "Who do you think taught the rest of them how?"

And you didn't think to mention this before?

Seth turned quietly to Asher, wary of being touched again.

"What *is* a portal?" he murmured.

"It's a gateway, dear boy!" The old woman clapped her hands suddenly, leading them down the ladder to one of the firmer patches of soil. "A magical door to a different place in the universe."

She lifted her eyes dreamily to the heavens.

"Out of place...out of time..."

The shifter glanced at the others in alarm. "Out of *time*? What does that—"

"Don't listen to her," Evie said grudgingly. "It's a door. A magic door that can open to any place we wish to go." Her eyes flashed. "Which *apparently* she's been able to do this *whole time*!"

Evianna brightened with a smile. "I'm sorry, dear. Was there a question in that?"

"*Why?*" the princess snapped. "Why in the *world* would you only be telling us about this now?! I don't care how differently time is moving, the fate of the realm is at stake!"

"It's not that simple," the witch replied.

"It's not that simple," Ellanden said at the same time. He flushed under the gaze of the others, looking incredibly reluctant to agree with her on any point. "My gran can do this kind of thing, but she rarely would. The same way you can't walk up to any random witch in the kingdoms and receive a prophecy on command. These things need to happen in their own time."

The witch's eyes twinkled. "There it is—that Kreo blood. I knew you had a little after all."

His eyes swept over her coldly, lingering on the webbing of shawls. "There's a chance you've begun to mold."

Asher shoved him for silence, and Cosette stepped forward with a touch of nerves. Despite her fragile looks, the girl didn't scare easily. But she'd avoided addressing the old witch directly so far. Perhaps the sight of such a person made her long for happier times. Perhaps she'd simply spent the last two years hearing horror stories of a similar such character from her best friend.

"Can you make one for us now?" she asked tentatively. "Can you send us to the Dunes?"

A swell of emotion bubbled in Evie's chest, catching her unawares and making it suddenly difficult to breathe. Was such a thing actually possible? After so long toiling away on the road, were they finally about to reach their destination? She glanced instinctively at the trees around her, scanning for supplies. They had very little in terms of weaponry. Hardly a single working blade.

"The Dunes," Asher repeated, caught in a similar state. The journey had seemed so indefinite a part of him didn't think they'd ever actually arrive. "A portal could take us there?"

Yes—it could.

Ellanden's great-grandmother had created a similar gateway, sending an army of rebels straight to the High Kingdom to storm the castle gates. All so Evie's mother could kill her twin.

...my family's a bit strange.

But magic didn't happen freely. It always came with a catch.

"Best not to dwell on specifics," Evianna answered in a sing-song voice, rummaging in her pockets and fishing out a pair of stones. "It will take you exactly where you need to be..."

"No, no, no!" Ellanden took a compulsive step forward, looking ready to tear the rocks right out of her hands. "Listen, crazy, we *need* to reach the Dunes. If you could send us there, it would be incredibly helpful. If not—"

"It isn't about the journey," the witch interrupted with a cackle. "It's about how many pieces you'll end up in along the way."

The fae stepped back, shaking his head. "I hate this place..."

The stones struck together and a glittering silver archway appeared in their place. Melting like the drips of a paintbrush until the ends buried into the spongy earth on either side.

"Seven hells," Evie gasped in spite of herself, then took a step forward.

The portal itself was clouded, but the edges were singing—a strange metallic sound, like someone sharpening a blade. She lifted a hand towards it, then glanced back nervously at the witch.

"Where does it lead?"

The smile remained, but for once the witch's eyes were serious. Staring at them with an odd, fixed quality—like a portrait come to life.

Or maybe we're the portrait, Evie thought with a shiver. *Maybe this is how she'll remember us; maybe she knows we're never coming back.*

"I don't know where it leads," she said quietly, looking at each one in turn. "But I do know the only way out of this place is for you to take those next few steps."

She warmed with a parting smile, nodding them forward.

"And now, my darlings...it's time for you to leave."

※

WHEN EVIE WAS A CHILD, she had forced her parents to tell the story. Threatening them when needed with childlike violence, memorizing each word as she drifted to sleep in their arms.

They were better than the books. They had been there in person. Full of fresh anecdotes and colorful details and forgotten conversations. No accounting was ever exactly the same.

She had easiest access to her parents, but Cassiel was the prize.

The Fae were natural born storytellers, and her uncle had endless patience for that kind of thing. More times than she could possibly remember she'd close her eyes and let his musical voice carry her away—painting fantastical pictures and taking her to places she'd never seen.

She remembered his description of the portal quite clearly. A magical doorway of sparks. In her mind, it had been an unearthly kind of beautiful. Like stepping through a waterfall, or waking from a peaceful dream. The transition was never jarring, it was illuminating. A picture come to life.

The reality was somewhat different.

"Seven hells!"

It was impossible to know who was the first one to curse, and both Asher and Seth fell to their knees at the same time. The witch followed shortly after, wrapping her arms around her stomach and gasping for breath. The princess was right on her heels.

"Look out!"

One world vanished behind her as the next slammed suddenly into view. Like squeezing through the neck of a bottle she felt all the air compress from her lungs, wringing her like a wet rag. Until finally, after her entire body was screaming, she plopped unceremoniously on the other side.

"Asher!"

She called for him instinctively, then buried her face in her hands. The world was spinning and she wanted no part of it. A wave of nausea stirred her stomach and she lay down on the ground.

Just kill me now...get it over with.

There was a sizzle as the portal sealed shut—just seconds after the fae swept under the arch.

For a split second, they were genuinely surprised—staring at their fallen comrades with a look of confusion, not understanding what had possibly gone wrong. Then that genetic pride kicked in and they started smiling, gazing down with the imperious expression so typical of their kind.

"Oh, Landi...they're hurting," Cosette said with mock concern, resting her boot on Freya's back. "We should find them some help."

The prince knelt beside Asher, petting the top of his head with a wicked smile.

"They're not hurting, Cousin, they're just not very good at standing." He smoothed the dark hair, then pushed lightly to his feet. "We'll have to show them after they catch their breath—"

In hindsight, the vampire may have overreacted a little.

"Bloody hell—Asher!" Ellanden cried, falling to the ground in a spray of blood. "I was *teasing,* you impossible psychopath!" He lifted a hand to his newly torn stiches, feeling suddenly dizzy himself. "Now you've killed me..."

Asher straightened up gingerly, looking not the slightest bit ashamed.

"That'll do you some good," he panted, a hand to his temple, "to die a little. I can't imagine anything else penetrating that thick skull."

"How about your hand?" the fae sulked, dabbing at the blood. "That's pretty effective—"

"Would you *stop*?" Evie commanded, pushing carefully to her knees. "Where are we?"

The friends lifted their heads a few inches off the ground, squinting. It wasn't a swamp, that much was clear. But aside from that, there wasn't a lot to go on.

There were trees, and more trees, and more trees...

We should have asked Evianna to give us a map.

"I'm going out on a limb...and say it's a forest."

It was quiet a moment, then the friends looked at Seth.

He was propped up on his elbows like the rest of them, peering speculatively into the trees. When he saw them looking, he shrugged defensively and gestured around with a wave of his hand.

"One might call it the woods."

With an even mix of laughter and profanity, the friends pushed shakily to their feet. Testing their balance with a little surge of confidence before promptly collapsing once more.

"I know I tend to criticize your skills as a guide," Ellanden muttered, watching as the others stumbled and fell, "but you really don't give yourself enough credit."

It was the same general time as when they'd left, that much was clear. The sun was still burrowing somewhere in the east and the ground was coated in dew. It wasn't yet mid-day.

But the woods themselves? A lovely, if generic, combination of fir and pine, with a soft carpet of moss and needles. No different than a thousand places they'd been before. No different than a thousand places they'd go again. If it weren't for a withered ivory trunk twisting out of the ground, a single differentiating feature, Evie could have drawn it by hand.

"This is fantastic," she muttered, stumbling away from the others to perch in the desiccated remains. Her stomach was heaving and it helped to be a little off the ground. "Heaven forbid the witch sends us where we need to go. Much better that she drops us off in, you know...*the woods*."

The others agreed, but were too weary to smile. Freya was still splayed out on the ground, squeezing her eyes shut and taking measured breaths. Asher had made it to a tree of his own, holding tight to the lower branches for balance, his pale skin even whiter than usual.

Only Seth was staring around the clearing, a strange emotion stirring in his eyes. "There's no limit to these portals?" he asked quietly. "They can really take you anywhere?"

The rest of the friends didn't hear him, or rather they were in no condition to respond.

"What's happening?" Asher moaned softly, tightening his grip on the tree so severely that wooden shavings crumbled off in his hand. "I can't...the ground is spinning."

Ellanden smiled faintly but the teasing had stopped, either out of a deeply-repressed sweetness of character or the fact that he was losing a borderline alarming amount of blood—it wasn't clear.

"Just a touch of mortality—breathe through it."

"Anywhere?" Seth repeated, though no one was listening. "It can take you anywhere?"

"This happened the last time," Cosette said softly, helping Freya to her feet. "Portals are difficult to travel, but only for a select group of people. My father said it took the most of the army over an hour to recover—men, shifters, vampires—all of them alike. But the fair folk were fine."

"The fair folk," Evie repeated with a derisive snort. "I can't believe you still—"

"*Answer me.*"

The others looked up in alarm as Seth pushed up from his knees and staggered to his feet, staring wildly around the clearing. His eyes rested a moment on the ghostly tree where Evie had perched before flying suddenly higher to find the faint outline of mountains in the distance.

"I don't believe it..." he murmured. "This can't be real."

By now, the friends were watching closely. They'd been thrown enough surprises to be wary of them now. But stunned as he was, there was nothing in Seth's face to make them worry.

On the contrary...he was smiling.

"This place," Cosette began slowly, "you know it?"

The smile brightened, settling in his eyes. "I know it."

Evie and Asher shared a quick look.

"Is there shelter?" he asked tentatively. "A place we could stay?"

Seth rotated in a slow circle, warming with an expression they hadn't yet seen. "...follow me."

Chapter 7

The friends might have been wandering before at a traveler's pace, new to the land and unsure where they were going, but all that was behind them now. Seth moved with a new sense of purpose, striding deliberately through the trees, eyes always on the next mountain.

He hadn't said a word to anyone, and despite their curiosity none of them was inclined to ask. Something about his expression silenced those burning questions, and they obediently followed several paces behind, trying to shake the dizziness, watching the back of his head.

After about thirty minutes Asher reached down suddenly, taking the princess' hand.

"How are you feeling?" he murmured.

She pulled in a deep breath, never breaking her stride. "Oh, you know...like I got sucked through a magical portal and got dumped half a world away." Their eyes met and she flashed a sweet smile. "How are *you* feeling?"

He laughed softly, draping an arm around her shoulder. "About the same. Maybe with a couple extra bruises along the way."

Ellanden flipped him off and kept walking.

"But you never told me," the vampire's fingers twirled absentmindedly, playing with a lock of her hair, "what did Evianna say to you last night?"

The princess shot him a reflexive glance and her heart skipped a beat—a tell she wished very much that he wasn't able to hear. It took only a second to recover, then she flashed another smile.

"Not much," she answered lightly. "She told me we were chosen for a reason." *She told me I was probably going to die.* "She told me everything was going to work out fine."

Asher studied her in silence before nodding quickly when she caught his eye. "Yeah, she was just...a ray of sunshine."

It was quiet for a few minutes as both stared into the distance, walking in silence. A lot more troubled than either was letting on. Their fingers were laced, but stiff. Her short strides never seemed to match his longer ones. It had gotten to a breaking point, when he turned again to her suddenly.

"Evie, is there something—"

"We're here."

The friends looked up in surprise as Seth came to an abrupt stop, staring through the forest towards what looked like a small clearing beyond the trees. His lips were parted and his breath was coming in quick bursts. Every part of him was humming with anticipation. Every part was straining to get closer. But for the life of him, he couldn't seem to move.

After a few seconds Cosette took a step forward, gently placing a hand on his arm.

"We're here?" she echoed softly.

He nodded in silence, unable to tear his eyes away. "I can't..."

The beaming smile was gone, leaving a look of quiet panic in its place. He faltered a few seconds then glanced back suddenly, as if he could still see the magical arch.

"I don't know why it took us here. I'm not—"

She slipped her hand into his. "How about we go a little farther?"

He glanced down suddenly, looking first at their fingers and then into her eyes. His gaze lingered there a moment, finding a solace he didn't yet realize himself.

Then he pulled in a deep breath and headed out of trees.

◈

IT WAS A VILLAGE.

A far different kind of village than what Evie was used to, but a village all the same.

This one was small, quiet—with no roads or major structures of any kind. Just a centralized well which seemed to be the social rallying point, circled by a few dozen primitive-looking houses. The kind that were built quickly, by unskilled hand, but tended to with an unusual amount of love.

Clusters of wildflowers grew in every window. Hand-stitched clothes were hanging on nearby trees to dry. Several fires had been lit, though it wasn't quite cold enough yet to merit them, and the smell of smoke-charred sausage and chicory drifted through the air.

As a child of castles and sprawling country estates, it was unlike anything the princess had ever seen. Her parents made it a point not to shelter her from the more impoverished areas of the realm. They'd visited them often, but never had she been somewhere so isolated and remote.

There was no way to approach it casually. The second they stepped beyond the tree-line, what felt like the entire village froze.

Women hovered over kettles of steaming water. A swarm of children paused in the middle of a game of chase. A trio of old men drifted out onto one of the porches—all of them staring in the same direction, trying to determine whether the group of battered teenagers posed a threat.

Then a lone woman peeled herself out of the crowd.

"...Seth?"

In a flash, the panic vanished and his entire body warmed to life.

"Mom!"

He raced forward with a euphoric bark of laughter, pausing only for a quick kiss before scooping her up in his arms. The friends watched in astonishment as he rotated in a slow circle, eyes closed, smiling beatifically, leaning in every few seconds to sniff her hair as she wept openly into his neck.

"I don't understand," she gasped when he finally set her down, lifting trembling hands to his cheeks. "Jack said you wouldn't be back for months. Where's the rest of the pack?"

Seven hells...she doesn't know.

Seth paused for a split second before turning her to face the others. "Mom, these are my friends."

The group lifted their hands in an awkwardly comical wave as her bright eyes swept over them, taking in the smallest details while keeping a firm grip on her son. After a few seconds, her face broke into a welcoming smile—a smile endearingly reminiscent of the young shifter himself.

"It's a pleasure to meet you. Any friends of Seth's are most welcome in the village." She lifted a hand, waving them closer. "Please—come warm yourselves by the fire."

<hr />

WHEN SHE FIRST MET Seth the princess remembered thinking there was a lot she liked about him, and a lot more she was unwilling to say. Well—that was the *second* time she met him. The first time, he was robbing them with a gang of cutthroats in the middle of a bar.

In the time since then, she had often wondered about his story. What little she knew was tragic—dead father, conscripted to work in the Red Hand, sold into gladiatorial slavery by his uncle. But none of that accounted for the man who travelled with her day after day.

The one who smiled with little provocation, who sang under his breath and made sure everyone else had enough to eat before sitting down himself. The one who risked his life without a moment's pause to help a band of people he barely even knew, who returned priceless pieces of jewelry and stole a kiss from the girl of his dreams before watching her ride away.

That man was raised somewhere different. *That* man was loyal to different kinds of people.

Looking around, it made sense that place would be here.

Just at a glance, Seth's village was poor. The kind of poor that made it difficult to notice anything else on the second or third glance. Until that day, it had never occurred to the princess that the condition came in degrees. That he might consider the Kreo village 'not poor' just because they had a connecting network of bridges and easier access to food. His own home was different.

The kind of place where you were always a little cold. Always a little hungry.

Coincidentally, it was filled with some of the kindest people Evie had ever met.

In addition to things like pavement and shoes, strangers were an absolute novelty to the village. The friends couldn't go two steps without someone new coming up for an introduction, offering some proud or funny story about the shifter—telling it in such a way that always guaranteed to make him blush. Time and time again, they were offered breakfast. This from people who barely had enough for their own plates. By the time they reached the final house, everyone of royal blood was secretly planning some kind of financial intervention. They'd complete the mission, return to their respective kingdoms, then bombard the little village with blankets and bread.

Cosette's gesture with the diamond necklace must have just astonished him, Evie realized, glancing between the shifter and the fae. *There's no reference point to help him understand.*

Kindness—yes. Generosity—yes. A kind of selflessness that always seemed to define those people who'd been given the least. But the grandiosity of the thing? Taking a string of gemstones and giving it to the slavers to set him free? She'd never forget the look on his face.

"And this is it," he stated, completing the tour with a self-conscious wave of his hand. "My house."

There was deep affection in every memory, a fierce protectiveness in the way he addressed people, in the things he pointed out. But aside from the witch his new friends had grown up in castles and finery. They had never seen a place such as this. He was secretly terrified what they might think.

Two people in particular.

"It isn't much," he murmured, casting a quick look at both of the fae. "It used to be a little bigger, but there was a fire a few years back—"

"It's wonderful," Ellanden interrupted unexpectedly. Cosette nodded behind him, dark eyes warming with a smile. He lifted a hand to the wooden beams. "Did you build it yourself?"

The shifter froze in surprise before nodding quickly. "Yes, I mean...my father did. I was too young to really help—"

Before he could finish, the door opened and three screaming children blurred outside.

It was a trio of dark-haired girls—ranging somewhere between two and ten—each wearing variations of the same threadbare dress. Their feet were bare and the ground was slick, but none of them seemed bothered by the chill. Their only focus was the man in front of them.

There was a whooping shriek as the two older ones threw themselves on top of him, clinging to his back like monkeys. The youngest hurried after them as best she could, but walking was still new and she couldn't keep up. Evie's heart melted immediately at the tiny chestnut curls.

"Always so dramatic with the entrance," he chided, but he was grinning from ear to ear. "These are my sisters—Anessa, Chloe, and Violet." His voice warmed with the last one and he scooped her off the ground. "Girls, these are some friends I met on the road."

As abruptly as they'd appeared the girls were suddenly shy, staring at the gang with eyes that didn't see travelers often. The littlest clung tightly to his neck, pressing her cheek to his.

Evie took a tentative step forward. "It's so nice to meet you."

She smiled at each of them, trying to coax little smiles in return. The rest of her friends were doing their very best to look non-threatening—mostly this involved checking for dried blood and discreetly hiding any blades. Just on principle, the vampire was standing near the back.

Three pairs of dark eyes followed their every move.

"Pretty strange, huh?" Seth teased, giving the youngest a little squeeze. "Wouldn't you like to introduce yourself?" The girl considered a split second, the shook her head quickly and buried her face in his neck. "Are you sure?" He winked at Cosette. "That one's a princess. And a fae."

That produced a reaction.

The little girls let out a collective gasp of astonishment while the friends exchanged a quick look. Their first instinct was panic, but in reality there was nothing to fear. They'd ventured to a place beyond the reaches of a map and were clearly the first visitors in quite some time. It didn't matter if the girls screamed it to the rooftops, their secret would still be safe.

"Is that true?" Chloe asked shyly, clinging to her brother's neck. "Is she really a princess?"

Cosette blushed, averting her gaze.

"Mmm-hmm." Seth's eyes twinkled with a smile. "Would you like to meet her?"

The children brightened at the same time, and curiosity had almost won over panic, when a clear voice called out from several paces behind.

"I see you wasted no time in strangling your brother."

After quite a bit of effort, Seth's mother extracted herself from the crowd and joined them at the far end of the village. Apparently, the young shifter's arrival was causing quite a stir. Even more so because he'd come without the rest of the pack. But whatever questions they had would have to wait until later. For the moment, there wasn't a force on earth that could tear her away from her son.

"Give him some space," she laughed, shooing the girls away. "The boy's dead on his feet!"

Evie pursed her lips with a secret smile.

Dead on his feet? This is the best we've looked in quite some time.

Seth raked his hair back with a blush. "And you already met my mother, Charlotte."

She flashed them all another smile, but she only had eyes for her son. One hand swept back his hair, while the other gripped his cloak. As if at any moment their fortunes might change and he'd vanish into the woods once again.

"I can't believe you're actually..." She trailed off with tears in her eyes, unable to finish. "I don't know why you're back, but I hope you can stay a few weeks? A few days?"

His face fell ever so slightly as he took her hand. "Actually, I don't think—"

"We can stay for a few days."

The rest of them turned to Evie in surprise, but none more so than Seth himself. For a split second, he looked afraid to hope. He recovered himself quickly.

"We can?" he ventured. "That would be all right?"

The princess lifted her shoulder with a grin. "The witch told us the portal would take us wherever we needed to go. There's a reason we're here. I don't know what that is yet...but one way or another we're going to find out."

There was a murmur of agreement from the others. Seth was breathless with delight. Only his mother seemed to think there was anything strange about that statement. She looked from one to the next, hoping someone would clue her in, before finally turning back to her son.

"The *witch* told you about the *portal*...?" she quoted, lifting her eyebrows in a way that made everyone present feel about two feet tall. "You and I need to have a little talk..."

Chapter 8

As it turned out, that little talk would have to wait. Whether it was their time in the swamp or portal-travel, as Freya had taken to calling it, the trip had taken a far heavier toll than any of the friends had realized. So within just a few minutes of being welcomed into Seth's childhood home, the entire gang found themselves drifting off to sleep.

By the time they came round, the sun had already set and a delicious aroma was drifting out of the kitchen. They awoke to a clatter of dishes, followed by a cheerful apology as Charlotte bustled back and forth, getting things ready. That being said, some awoke easier than others.

Asher opened his eyes to find two-year-old Violet just an inch away from his face.

"Do you need a bandage?"

He pulled back quickly, staring in surprise. "...I'm sorry?"

The girl reached out a finger, touching a gash on his arm. "You're bleeding."

There was another clatter of dishes in the kitchen, and Evie suddenly wondered if Charlotte realized what Asher was. She remembered Seth's condemnation of vampires when they'd met. He hadn't seen one in person, but in the last few years their atrocities had become well known.

He glanced down in surprise. Her finger pulled away red.

"*Violet!*" The woman swooped in and grabbed the girl, flashing a wary look at the vampire that she quickly turned into a tight smile. "Let's just...get you cleaned up. Okay, sweetie?"

Without another word she rushed the child outside to the well, washing her finger in the icy water again and again and again.

Yes...she definitely knows.

Asher froze on the couch, head bowed, gingerly cupping his arm. The others shot each other a look then moved past it, each of them pretending not to notice what was going on.

The princess waited until they were talking, then crossed the room to the vampire's side.

"Do you need to feed?" she murmured, perching on the sofa beside him.

He flashed her a quick look, then dropped his gaze to the floor. "I think that would probably unsettle people further."

She raised her eyebrows. "More than you bleeding on the couch?"

When he said nothing she took him by the hand and led him quickly from the house, circling around back until was nothing around them but trees. The second they were alone she rolled up her sleeve and offered her arm, keeping an eye on the village the entire time.

"Be quick about it," she murmured, peering towards the fires. "The last thing we want is an angry mob with pitchforks marching over to save my life."

He stared at her in silence.

"...too soon?"

With a reluctant sigh he lifted her wrist, but hesitated a second before he bit down.

"Are you sure?" he asked softly. "I never want to just presume—"

"It's fine. I'm sure." She glanced over in spite of herself, shivering when his cool breath touched her bare skin. "Just...not too hard."

He paused an inch away, lips curving into a smile.

"Not too hard?" he repeated. "It has to be a *little* hard."

"Well, I know that—"

"That's kind of the whole point."

"Okay, you know what I—"

"It has to break the skin."

"Would you stop?" she demanded. "I'm aware! Just drink so we can get back inside and *I* can have some dinner. Portal travel has me starved."

He snorted with laughter. "Don't call it that..."

Considering the lengthy wind-up, the moment was over rather fast.

Using as little force as possible, Asher bit down gently until he found a vein. A sudden pressure laced up the inside of the princess' arm, but it was over almost as soon as it had begun—leaving him flushed and panting, while she shivered in the frosty night.

"That's it?" she asked in surprise. "Are you sure?"

He nodded quickly, rolling down her sleeve. "That's all I need."

She blinked as he pressed a sudden kiss to her lips, lingering there as his eyes danced in the silver light. He pressed another to her wrist and headed back to the cabin, waiting for her outside the door. She walked past him obliviously, surprised when he pulled her back once again.

"Wh—"

His lips came down over hers, coaxing them open with a little smile. A strange time for a kiss, perhaps. But blood did strange things to vampires. And it had been far too long.

"Tell me again why we're here," he murmured, slipping his tongue into her mouth when she tried to reply. "Why didn't we just stay at the castle, enjoy the party..."

That's a bloody good question.

Her head was spinning and she couldn't seem to remember the answer. When it finally came back to her, the most she could do was fire it out in breathless, choppy fragments.

"Poison. Prophecy. Fire and brimstone." She pulled back an inch with a grin, holding fistfuls of his shirt. "Eternal damnation if we happen to fail."

He scoffed and tossed back his hair. "Eternal damnation. You'd be surprised how often I've been threatened with that."

She smiled breathlessly, balanced on the tips of her toes.

It didn't matter that they were standing on a stranger's porch, in full view of the village, after magically transporting on a mission to save the realm. The only thing that registered was the man in front of her. The one who was standing a little too close, tilting his head with a bewitching smile.

I might be willing to trade a little damnation for this...

Asher seemed to be thinking the same thing.

"All right—hear me out on this." He kissed the tip of her nose, bending lower to catch her eyes. "You could argue *timing*, sure, that's reasonable." Another wet kiss, stealing the breath right from her lungs. "But we're new and I think...I think there should be a lot more kissing."

Amongst other things.

She smiled in spite of herself, wrapping her arms around his neck.

"I agree about the kissing. *Lots* more kissing." She teased her lips an inch from his, leaning back when he tried to move closer. "But do you really want to stay on this freezing porch, watching your girlfriend starve to death all because you wanted to make out?"

He dug his hands into his pockets with a sigh. "No I'd much rather go inside, where everyone thinks I was about to eat that little girl..."

She flashed him a grin, pulling open the door. "Not *eat* her, Asher. Maybe just maim her a little bit."

By the time the pair made it back inside, dinner was fully underway. Most of the food was already plated and on the table, while Charlotte was busy ferrying the rest. She paused only once to cheerfully oust the Prince of the Fae from the kitchen. Something she'd already done two times.

"Please, let me help you," Ellanden said again, watching helplessly as she breezed back and forth. The woman had clearly emptied her entire pantry to prepare enough food for the table, and the fae had half a mind to sneak away and hunt. "You've already been more than generous—"

She held up a silencing hand, ushering him out to the living room. "You brought my boy home. The least I can do is cook you dinner."

"I wouldn't try to argue with her," Seth called from the sofa, watching the exchange with a knowing smile. "You'll never win."

Ellanden grinned faintly, then sat down beside him.

There wasn't much to the house, nothing like what he was used to. At one point, it had probably been a single large room that had been quartered off with late-coming walls and awkward extensions as the family grew. From his perch on the sofa, the fae was able to see almost the entire cabin. But his bright eyes flew from one thing to the next, memorizing details, curious all the same.

"You never told me you had sisters," he said quietly, watching the girls across the room.

Seth followed his gaze with a shrug.

"You never asked." His dark eyes warmed affectionately, following Violet as she made her way across the floor. The hem of her dress trailed behind her. "Anyway, I hadn't seen them in a long time. That one wasn't even walking when I left."

As if she heard them, the little girl veered suddenly to the sofa—toddling proudly towards them. Both men warmed at the same time. Seth lifted his arms as Ellanden forgot all dignity and slipped to the floor, waving her forward encouragingly.

Evie watched with a secret smile.

In her experience, it was always the men who were best with a sword that were the most charmed by children. She supposed there was a joke to be made in that somewhere.

Violet reached the sofa and crawled into Seth's lap, reaching up immediately to play with his dark braids. A second later, she noticed the fae's hair was strung with them as well.

"You, too?" she squeaked in delight.

He leaned forward with a smile, letting her touch. "Me, too."

Seth watched with amusement. "Aw...look at that," he said caustically. "We have so much in common."

"Manners," his mother chided, swatting his head as she breezed past. "We can't have them thinking we're *completely* uncivilized."

He flashed a grin. "Their manners are worse than mine."

She smiled indulgently, then waved the rest of them closer. "Come to the table—the food's getting cold."

<hr />

EVIE WASN'T SURE WHAT family dinners were normally like in the little village, but judging by the expression on the children's faces she was fairly sure they were seated at some kind of feast. It was simple food—biscuits, vegetables, potatoes—but it was deliciously prepared and there was plenty to go around. A pair of candles burned low on the table as the friends passed the dishes back and forth, kicking back in their chairs and telling stories by the light of a dancing fire.

"—so we ended up inviting the troll to come with us," Freya described as she speared another biscuit, jerking a finger at Cosette, "but then *this* one decided at the last minute she didn't want to swim."

The table roared with laughter as the lovely fae shook her head.

"In the middle of winter? To an imaginary tree-house?" She gave the witch an exasperated smile. "No, Freya. I didn't want to swim."

There was another burst of raucous laugher as the little girls whispered to each other in amazement. Their older brother was staring across the table with a secret smile.

"Swimming with cave trolls, huh?" His eyes twinkled over the rim of his glass. "Don't know why I'd be surprised..."

Cosette dropped her eyes with a blush, while Ellanden glanced between them irritably.

"Should never have involved a troll in the first place," he muttered disapprovingly. "Filthy beasts, every single one. I don't know why you'd attempt something so reckless."

Asher and Evie kicked him at the same time, while Cosette gave him a choice look.

"For the sake of irony, how about *you* don't give lectures on what it means to be reckless."

He shrugged stiffly. "I don't know what you mean."

Evie kicked him again.

"So in a single meal, I think we've covered everything from cave trolls to experimental hair styling." Charlotte's eyes twinkled as they went from her eccentric houseguests to her son. "Everything except the basics. Where did you all meet?"

A sudden hush fell over the table.

That's a good question...

Her gaze jumped from one to the other, but the friends clammed up at the same time. It wasn't meant to be a difficult question. She was probably just surprised they hadn't mentioned it before. A look of confusion washed over her before she hesitantly tried again.

"Where are you going?"

Silence.

Evie shot a quick look at Seth.

It was his silence. It was his mother asking the question.

But he hadn't planned on coming home. Hadn't planned on being faced with such a conversation. He hadn't yet confronted what had happened himself. A flicker of true panic lit his eyes, and for the life of him he didn't know what to say.

Charlotte stared at them for a moment.

"All right...let's try something easier. What business brings you together?"

The silence had overtaken them, hovering in the cabin like an unwanted cloud. But after only a few seconds, Evie lifted her head in a sudden burst of inspiration.

"Oh—Seth's our guide!"

The tension cracked as each of the friends quickly leapt on board, echoing different versions of the same answer with almost comical speed. All except one. Evie kicked Ellanden under the table.

"He's a...fantastic guide."

Charlotte nodded slowly, fighting back a smile.

She knew how to read between the lines, how to tell when a group of teenagers was evading. She knew her son was supposed to be with his uncle and the rest of the pack, and she knew well enough to be certain when something was wrong.

But he was here. He was safe. He was sitting amongst a group of people he obviously trusted and admired. And she couldn't help but notice how, every few seconds, his eyes stole to the beautiful girl sitting across the table.

As long as he was smiling...the rest of it could wait.

"A fantastic guide?" she quoted, lifting the nearest platter and passing it along. "This from a boy who couldn't find his way home unless he wrote the directions on his hand?"

The table fell silent once again. This time, everyone was staring in the same direction.

Seth turned a particular shade of grey, while Ellanden looked with a genuine smile to their hostess—a woman who'd just found an eternal friend. The quiet stretched on a few more painful seconds, getting worse and worse, then Freya reached out discreetly and checked the shifter's palms.

The little girls burst out laughing. New candles were lit for another round.

Home sweet home.

DINNER THAT NIGHT LASTED far longer than anyone had planned—so long that Violet fell asleep right there at the table and had to be carried off to bed. The candles extinguished themselves and Charlotte pushed to her feet, gathering the plates from across the table. At any rate, she tried.

"Please—let me." Ellanden rose swiftly, taking the dishes out of her hands. "It's the least I can do, after you cooked such a delicious meal."

Having learned his lesson the first time, he didn't wait for her to refuse. He simply took what he could carry and headed outside to the well. The door swung shut behind him.

"All right, girls." She turned to her remaining daughters, both of whom were having trouble coming down from the excitement of the day. "Time for bed—say goodnight to everyone."

They dug their heels in immediately, turning to their brother instead.

"Will you read us a story?"
"Please, Seth...please?"
Charlotte shook her head sternly.
"Your brother is very tired—"

"I'll do it." Cosette stepped forward with a smile then froze uncertainly as the little family turned to stare at her, one hand still reaching out for the book. "I mean...may I?"

Seth stared in shock as the girls squealed in delight, leading the princess down the crooked hallway. A second later, his eyes drifted outside to where the prince was cleaning dishes in the well.

"...what the heck is happening right now?"

Asher laughed softly, settling back on the couch. "You've only seen them in less than hospitable conditions, so I'll just tell you...Fae are obsessed with the idea of home."

"Just one of a thousand neurotic compulsions," Evie added authoritatively. "For the good of the realm, the entire civilization should be psychoanalyzed then put to sleep."

The shifter's eyes flickered involuntarily around the tiny cabin. "...home?"

Asher smiled again, kinder this time. "Admittedly, in their case that usually implies an ivory castle in a starlit forest—but home is home. They know it when they see it."

Seth nodded slowly, staring down the hall.

The princess was reading from a book of fairytales, her voice rising and falling like music, his little sisters gathered on either side. At some point, Violet had joined them—squirming her way beneath the book to nestle in the fae's lap.

The shifter drew in a quiet breath, immortalizing the image in his mind.

Then a door shut loudly behind him.

"All finished." Ellanden set down the plates with an extra flourish, shattering the tender moment. He smiled pointedly at the shifter. "Where should we go to sleep?"

For one of the first times, Seth held his gaze.

"There's a schoolhouse no one uses anymore, just across the courtyard."

A clear dismissal. But Ellanden stayed right where he was.

"Show me?"

A direct question. Asked in front of his mother.

The shifter had no choice but to comply.

With a frustrated sigh, he pulled on his cloak and kissed Charlotte on the cheek with a quiet murmur of explanation. He swept to the door a second later, knocking into the fae on the way out.

"What is wrong with you?" Evie hissed as she followed behind.

The prince fastened his own cloak with a look of total innocence.

"What? Because I asked where we should sleep?"

She rolled her eyes and stepped outside. Asher followed with a punishing hiss.

THAT NIGHT THE SIX friends hunkered down in a one-room schoolhouse that, from the looks of things, had been deserted for quite some time. The shelves were empty and stains leaked down from the windows. A cluster of primitive desks had been shoved into the corner; most of them were missing large pieces, as if at one point or another they had been used to build a fire.

It was cold, but it was dry. Under the circumstances, it was more than they could ask for.

"I wonder what happened here," Freya murmured, poking through some abandoned supplies. The floorboards were stained with flecks of ink and powdered chalk.

Evie glanced over curiously before peering out the window into the dark.

"You'll have to ask him..."

Seth's mother had silenced all those burning questions during dinner, but she was getting answers to them now. The two of them were perched on the edge of the well, lost in a deep and painful conversation. For the most part, she was crying. For the most part, he kept his eyes on the stone. At one point near the end she froze with a look of horror and took his wrist, pressing a silent kiss to a bite-shaped crescent on the back of his hand.

Evie stopped watching then.

"So why do you think we were meant to come *here*?"

Grateful as she was to have mended fences in the swamp, and touched as she was to see Seth reunited with his family, she was beginning to feel a bit like a leaf in the wind. Blown from one place to the next, with very little say as to where she was going.

The Dunes. They needed to get to the Dunes.

Why do the fates keep sending us the other way...?

The door opened and shut as Seth joined the rest of them—opting, out of loyalty, to forsake his room in the cabin and sleep with the others outside. He looked subdued, but strangely relieved as well. One hand kept drifting over to touch the fading warmth of his mother's kiss.

"Are you guys good out here?" he asked briskly, surveying the limited stockpile of blankets they'd pilfered from the house. "I could see if there's anything else—"

"This is fine," Evie said quickly, flashing a bright smile. "Better than fine. Seth...your family is amazing. I haven't had a dinner like that in a long time."

He shrugged dismissively, but she could tell he was pleased.

"Yeah, well...they don't get company very often. It was nice for them, too."

A door opened and shut in the distance as Cosette made her way across the courtyard.

"Did you tell your mother about the prophecy?" Ellanden asked curiously, unable to stop himself. "Is that what you were talking about so long?"

Seth glanced through the window at the princess before shaking his head. "We didn't talk about the prophecy. We actually just talked about you."

The friends paused in unison as the prince looked up in alarm.

"Me? Why would—"

"We were debating whether to drown you in the well."

They settled down for the night with a tempered burst of laughter, rearranging their blankets and clustering together as if they were still sleeping in a tent. The night was cold, but it was hard to feel it when Evie was nestled back in Asher's arms, still smiling at the shifter's dark humor.

That being said, she felt perfectly entitled to blame Seth for what happened next...

Chapter 9

The princess opened her eyes slowly, blank and uncertain, gazing up towards the heavens as waves of filtered sunlight rippled across her face. It was beautiful, she supposed. In a blinding kind of way. She lifted a hand to shield her eyes, watching as her hair drifted past like a fiery cloud.

Only then did she realize something was different.

Her body was useless, held in suspension, arms and legs too sluggish to respond to her commands. She wasn't breathless with surprise, she was literally unable to breathe—like someone was holding an invisible pillow over her face.

And she was cold. So bloody cold.

Perhaps because she was underwater.

Her mouth flew open in a silent scream that floated to the surface in a line of bubbles. The rest of the world carried on as if nothing had happened. Bits of algae and grass floated by on the current. Little creatures scuttled past her feet, which were impossibly buried in the sand.

There was a current...and her feet were touching the sand.

It was a river, then—not a lake or the sea. And what was more, she had the strangest feeling she knew it. That in some distant life, she'd stood on the very same riverbed once before.

Fascinating...but I'm about to drown!

There was movement on the shore above her, a sudden appearance of people making their way slowly out of the trees. It was hard to make out faces, to make out basic shapes, but a man and a woman were walking in front. Rather, the woman was walking. The man was kneeling down every few steps and pressing the tips of his fingers to the stone.

He's tracking someone, the princess realized.

She'd seen people move like that before. Most often when they were teaching her to move like that herself. A soft approach to a wild world. Violent things revealed only with a gentle hand.

A second later, she realized who those people were.

Her mouth opened in another scream, but her parents couldn't hear her. Nor could they seem to see her, though she was thrashing violently just a few inches below the crystal waves.

She watched instead, as there was nothing else to do.

She watched as her beautiful mother, frozen in youthful enchantment, stepped up beside her father, staring out over the waves. Her expression was colder than the water. Fear and horror and dread incarnate—it crept beneath the skin and burrowed into the young princess' bones.

Dylan, her father, touched her hand briefly, almost as if to ground himself, then knelt once again at the very edge of the shore. All the tracks stopped there. The wolves had told him the same thing. The guards had told him the same thing. All the tracks stopped there. But he had to see it for himself.

With an expression to rival her mother's, he reached out very slowly and dipped his fingers into the water—just a whisper away from his daughter's outstretched hands. A surge of emotion ripped across his face as he registered the intense cold, the dangerous speed.

Neither of which three fleeing teenagers could hope to survive.

His head bowed. The people behind him froze very still. And she realized, in a startling moment of clarity, it was the first time she'd ever seen her father cry.

She was still screaming for him when the image blurred away.

"DADDY—"

A burst of cold air hit her like a slap to the face, the watery picture vanishing as it cleared away into something else. Vampires weren't exactly warm by nature, but she and Asher had still managed to cocoon into something tolerable beneath their borrowed blankets—a thin layer of protection to shield them from the frosty night. That protection was quickly torn away.

There was sudden movement beside her. A blur of speed and a feral hiss.

Seth froze instinctively, his wrist imprisoned in Asher's deadly hand.

"Easy, vampire. I come in peace." He pulled away with a deliberately light smile, turning his eyes to the princess instead. "You up for a little run?"

She stared at him in silence, trying to make sense of her own head.

Whatever that was hadn't felt like a dream. It had felt like a memory. Which, of course was impossible, because while she was certain her parents had searched the river, the friends had been long gone. No, it wasn't a dream. But it wasn't a memory. It was something else entirely.

Something that was fading fast.

And his question...what was his question? Was she up for a run? No one who'd spent any amount of time with her would ever ask such a question. The princess' aversion to exercise was the bane of her Belarian father's existence—the only man who'd ever proposed such a thing himself.

My father...

"What?" she finally repeated, trying to circle back.

Seth's lips quirked in a grin as Asher retracted his fangs and fell back to the ground—pulling up the blankets with an expression that was part irritation, part smile. Mostly just cold.

"You want her to go for a run?" he mumbled, burrowing down until the only thing visible was the top of his head. "And people think I'm the dangerous one?"

She glanced down at him, wanting to deny it, then returned to the shifter with a shrug. "He's right. I'll kill you."

Without another thought she dropped back down beside him, desperate to tunnel inside and get a little of that warmth for herself. But with the same cheerful bluntness as when he'd forced her to shift on the ship, Seth grabbed her arm and heaved her upwards.

"Come on." He smoothed down her hair and started towing her briskly through the schoolhouse. "The others are waiting."

Her violent protests fell short on her tongue.

...the others?

There was no need to ask the question. The moment he pulled open the door, she was able to see for herself. No fewer than twenty other people were waiting in the muddy courtyard, wearing shockingly little clothing—their faces lit with matching anticipatory smiles.

She froze where she stood, abruptly overwhelmed. "Are they...are they hunting or something?"

Something practical. Something less animalistic than what she was envisioning. But Seth merely shook his head, slipping off his cloak and the shirt that was underneath.

Smart of him to do that AFTER stealing a vampire's girlfriend from his bed.

"Just a run. The weather's nice. We can stretch our legs a little."

She nodded quickly, or maybe she was just trembling. In a bizarre way, it reminded her of something Dylan would say himself. The weather's nice? There were five inches of ice on top of the well. He'd shake back his hair, eyes brimming with restless energy, while her mother would burrow deep inside their bed, mumbling something about dragon fire and wanting to keep all of her toes.

That being said, impending hypothermia was the least of Evie's worries.

"I'll just...uh..." She lowered her voice as the shifters talked quietly amongst themselves, well aware they'd be able to hear her anyway. "I'll just undress, then?"

Please let my friends not be watching.
Please let NO ONE be watching.

Seth's eyes softened, though most of that teasing smile remained. "Feeling shy?"

It was stupid, she was aware of this. Wolves didn't get shy. And royalty had nothing to do with it. Her father would strip down like all the rest of them and blur into the woods.

...his teenage daughter was a bit more hesitant.

She scoffed, tossing back her hair with an icy glare. "No, of course not."

I fault Ellanden for pride, but seriously, am I any better?

She unfastened her own cloak and folded it carefully, propping it up on what looked like a drier bit of stone. Her shoes were soon to follow, dropping her core temperature about a thousand degrees the moment her toes made contact with the frozen mud.

"Shy," she muttered again, cursing him for mentioning it, "that's utterly ridiculous."

But she grabbed the handsome shifter and positioned him like a shield, going against every social instinct she had and reaching up to unlace her dress. It fell with a whisper to the ground, set immediately on top of the cloak. For all the good it would do.

With my luck, it's going to rain.

Her hair tumbled long and free around her shoulders as he glanced behind him to see if she was ready, trailing like ribbons of fire along her pale skin. He tugged a lock with a good-natured grin.

"See—cover." He gestured to the men with a smile. "We don't have that."

"You don't have breasts, either."

"...that's a fair point."

That was the last of the talking.

Before the princess could say another word—ask where they were headed, how long they would be gone, if they might want to have breakfast instead—the people in the courtyard vanished, one after another, leaving a pack of restless wolves standing in their place.

Seth gave her a final look before doing the same.

It was still jarring—the speed of it, the casual way in which it was done. She was about to mention as much, when she abruptly realized she was the only naked person in the clearing.

Coincidentally, that made it *much* easier to shift.

The cold vanished the second she no longer had skin. As did the feeling that she was separate from the rest of them, somehow. That she was awkward, and misplaced, and standing in something cold. The instant her body transformed, most thoughts vanished as well. Well they didn't vanish so much as temper into something she could choose to entertain only if she wished. She felt herself irresistibly excitable, yet grounded—endowed with her father's coveted sense of calm.

Mostly, she felt ready. She felt ready for absolutely anything.

That was a good thing, too.

Because it would take everything she had to keep up with the pack...

HEAVEN...SIMPLY HEAVEN.

All her life the princess had imagined what it would be like, watching from the window of her father's palace as the royal guard shed their cloaks and tunics and sprinted in all their lupine brilliance into the woods. It was like watching a flock of birds—able to shift direction and turn at a moment's notice. Inexplicably precise synchronicity that baffled anyone who wasn't a part of it, and made subtle mockery of the fact that they were technically unable to speak.

They spoke to each other in different ways.

Come on—faster!

When it had first started, Evie was terrified she was going to lose them. She was disoriented, frantic, and gasping for breath. It wasn't until Seth slowed down, falling into pace beside her, that she realized things were steady, *she* was steady, and she was breathing just fine.

That's when she bit him on the shoulder, and leapt past with a euphoric howl.

The rest of the pack took it up immediately, calling back and forth like echoes of a bell as they streamed like a predatory flood through the trees. Each step was quicker than the last. Each bounding leap was thrilling and effortless. The ground compacted beneath each springing paw, and before long she found herself digging in with her claws—forcing herself even faster.

Seth appeared a step behind her, flying gracefully through the trees with each of his long strides. The princess glanced at him suddenly, struck by something she should have realized before.

He finally shifted.

It hadn't happened since he'd been attacked by vampires. After those who'd forced the bond claimed they wanted to know 'how it felt as a wolf', the shifter was half-convinced he'd never make the transformation again. He'd stayed human, even when it wasn't the better option. Even when he needed to fight. Even when he needed to heal. Yet looking at him now, he'd never been happier.

I guess sometimes we just need to come home.

The two shared a quick look, a secret smile, then he cocked his head ever so slightly behind them. She glanced back herself, truly astonished by what she saw.

No longer was she trailing near the back, appalled by her own fledgling clumsiness and trying desperately to keep up. She had surged through the ranks and was sprinting in the very front, setting the pace for the others, deciding which way they were going to go.

In a distant echo, Asher's words flashed through her mind.

'You're the Belarian princess. Everyone is in your pack.'

And this had to be a part of Belaria, did it not? The kingdom had many remote areas, and most shifters lived somewhere within its domain. The weather-beaten village, the little girls racing around the table at dinner...even Seth. Seth was one of her subjects.

She almost laughed at the thought. Such titles seemed utterly ridiculous as a wolf.

They were her pack. That's the only thing that mattered.

And my pack is getting ideas...

An unfortunate bed of ferns tore to pieces beside them as one of the larger, black wolves bounded suddenly to her side. He knocked heads quickly with Seth before turning her way with a look she realized was asking for permission. A little stunned she nodded, slowing her pace ever so slightly as he steered them in a different direction, flying like an arrow through the trees.

The forest, which she'd thought was just like any other when they'd crash landed from the swamp, was actually quite different than anything she was used to. Different in the way that no two places on earth are ever exactly alike. It was a patchwork. A clump of spruce here, a smattering of birch there. Tall white alders sprang up like punctuation from amidst the darker clusters of sequoia and pine. The princess spurred herself even faster, taking in everything at a glance. Tiny pink flowers dotted the moss, the kind people passed by without ever noticing. A wren sounded a sudden cry, and before she could turn to look the entire pack burst through an unexpected grove of hemlock.

There was beauty and danger. Blending together to create a picture all its own.

The wolves were panting now, digging their claws for extra traction as the ground steepened dramatically, leading them higher and higher up an alpine trail. The air was moist and cool, sounds of distant water echoing from somewhere just out of sight. Evie's nose sharpened with the scent and she craned her neck to see where it was coming from. But no sooner had the question materialized than the pack came to an abrupt stop—skidding dangerously on a ledge of thick stone.

The princess froze on instinct, then stepped forward in delight.

It's beautiful!

The climb must have been steeper and lengthier than she'd thought, because no longer were they in the wooded valley that Seth's people called home. They'd risen well above it to a place where mountain met sky. It stretched over them, blue and clear, while a river they'd been loosely following tumbled free of its confines and crashed in a dazzling drop over the cliff face.

It was the kind of place that took your breath away. The kind that made people do crazy things—make wild declarations, experience moments of stunning clarity, consider poetry, propose.

The princess warmed with a smile then glanced shyly at the wolf who'd led them, grateful he'd shared such an exquisite spot. But the wolves weren't much for sight-seeing. If anything they were revving themselves up, shivering with anticipation like something ready to explode.

She stared in confusion as one of the smaller ones swiftly moved backwards, bouncing in place the way she'd seen knights do the moment before a joust. Her eyes flickered quickly between the child and the others, wondering if anyone else had noticed.

Then, in a sudden burst of speed, the wolf launched itself forward...right over the cliff.

SEVEN HELLS!

She let out a wolfish scream, lurching forward.

There was no splash. The wolf was still falling. With a detached sort of horror she took one step after another, inching closer, staring over the staggering drop.

What should we do, she thought desperately, realizing for the first time how often she must wring her hands. *Why would they do such a thing? Should we try to—*

A body blurred past her. Then another, and another. With canine shrieks of delight the entire pack hurled themselves off the cliff, spiraling wildly before vanishing into the mist.

...I should have stayed in bed.

Faster than she would have thought possible, it was over. There were only two left. Just her and Seth, standing on the slick ledge. He glanced over the side, lips pulling back in a smile.

Oh no you don't!

Unable to scream as a person, she did her best as a wolf. Snarling and stomping and making all sorts of sounds she'd never heard, but translated quite clearly as rage.

He turned back slowly, lifting his eyes to her face.

This is the reason he brought me, she realized all at once. *From the first second we left the village, he knew we were going to end up here.*

Their eyes locked for one crystalline moment.

Then they heard a distant howl.

Seth's eyes lit up as he eagerly moved to the edge of the cliff, staring blindly into the chasm beyond. They were still dancing when he turned back to her with an imploring yip.

See? he seemed to say. *No one was hurt. They're calling to us.*

Evie wasn't sure how she was picking up on that so clearly. There was no such thing as canine telepathy. And truth be told, she and Seth didn't know each other all that well.

But it was clear he wanted to jump. He wanted her to jump, too.

No!

She shook her head quickly, prancing nervously in place. There was no shortage of ways she expected to die fulfilling this prophecy, but recreational cliff-diving wasn't on the list.

He cocked his head with a teasing smile, dancing backwards towards the falls.

Her eyes narrowed and a low growl whistled between her teeth. She might have been too late to stop the rest of them, but she wasn't going to let this idiot die in some freak adrenaline high.

She would kill him herself.

Don't. You. Dare.

There was no way to say the words out loud, but he seemed to intuit them nonetheless. A wicked smile danced in his eyes as he paced a step closer to the edge, daring her to stop him.

The growling intensified.

I command you!

If anything, he seemed to think it was funny. He barked once with laughter before clearing his expression to stare at her with wide, innocent eyes. Eyes that flashed with sudden panic when he ventured too close and his back paw slipped over the edge.

SETH!

She flew forward without thinking, desperate to catch him, baffled how to do such a thing without the use of her hands. Her heart pounded as her claws scrambled frantically across the flat rock. She was a second away from simply grabbing him with her teeth, when he pivoted abruptly and tackled her instead...sending them both flying off the ledge.

⁕

IT WAS IMPOSSIBLE TO really scream as a wolf, but the princess screamed anyway.

She screamed the whole way down.

It was a high unlike anything she'd ever felt. Flushing her skin and chilling her blood as she and Seth careened towards the churning water, spinning like jointless dolls in the air.

Her eyes snapped shut, but she forced them back open—determined to take in every terrifying second. Sounds and colors blended together. Her stomach rose with a giddy kind of weightlessness as a cloud of mist spiraled upward, tickling her ears and toes.

Seth dipped in and out of her vision. Depending on which way he was facing. Depending on which way she was facing. She had been determined to murder him, seized with grotesque plans.

But a second later...she forgave him instead.

This is AMAZING!

She let loose another euphoric howl.

How often had she teased Ellanden for this sort of thing? Asher despaired that the fae couldn't stay anywhere longer than ten minutes without trying to jump out to his death.

That might have been true. As a princess, she might have despaired as well.

But as a wolf...she wished it was even higher.

They hit the water with enough force to dent stone, streaking past the group of shifters on the shoreline and plummeting like two comets into the river. By all accounts, it was a great success.

Only one of them surfaced.

The other did not.

"Evie?" Seth wiped a hand of water from his face, breathless and smiling, still shaking off the effects of a quick transformation as he turned in a circle, searching for the princess. "Evie?"

His voice echoed quietly under the surface, distorted by the rippling waves, but the princess never heard it. The second she'd touched the freezing water, a kind of trance had taken hold.

As one had kicked towards the surface, the other had sank lifelessly into the depths.

My father...

The word hit her like a drug.

There was something about my father...

Her eyes fluttered open and shut, while her arms drifted out in front of her. The impact had triggered the shift in her as well, replacing that crimson fur with a tangle of slender limbs.

"Evie!"

Seth's smile had vanished and panic was taking hold. At first he'd thought she was kidding—getting him back for throwing her off the cliff in the first place. He'd waited for the sudden reappearance, for her to surface with a triumphant splash, laughing at the fear on his face.

But that window had all but closed. There was simply no sign of her.

"EVIE!"

He pulled in a deep breath and dove beneath the waves.

The princess was staring up at the rippling sunlight, oddly aware that she'd been in the same place just a short while before. Another part of her was convinced she'd never left—that she kept coming back there, time and time again. Floating in the ocean after the shipwreck, staring down from the railing as a chorus of distant voices echoed up from the sea.

My father searching...searching the water...

A strong hand closed around her wrist.

"Are you okay?" Seth didn't wait until they'd reached the shoreline to start shouting. The second their heads broke the surface, his voice began pounding in her brain. "Evie—talk to me!"

She tried, but it was difficult. Not only was she still reeling from the transition, but he wasn't giving her time to speak. No sooner had he fired out one question than he bombarded her with another.

"What happened?!" He dragged them onto the opposite shoreline as the others, gesturing them onwards with an impatient wave of his hand. "Did you hit your head on something? Everly, I'm so sorry! I never thought—"

She spat a mouthful of water into his face.

That's for tackling me.

He pulled back a few inches, too stunned to speak.

"I'm okay," she said reassuringly before shaking her head. "No, I'm not okay."

Their eyes locked together.

"Seth...I think I'm going to die."

Chapter 10

"I've been having these really strange dreams..."

The two shifters sat on the bank of the river, dripping pools of water into the soft grass. The rest of the pack had continued running without them—waved on by Seth's dismissive hand. But the jump off the cliff had shaken both to the core, and neither was in any state to be leaving.

"Dreams?"

Seth's eyebrows rose and he fought to keep an even voice.

Before he'd met his strange new friends, his life had been very different. The village was a daily onslaught of harsh realities. The kind of place where mistakes were costly, where people could die from being too hungry or too cold. Life with his uncle had been a different kind of grim, forcing him on the wrong side of confrontations he wanted nothing to do with, chipping away little pieces of his soul. Mistakes were costly there, too—answered with quick violence, paid in full with blood.

But his friends knew nothing of that side of the world. Their eyes were full of hope, their plans full of whimsy. Even when they were down in the trenches, fighting tooth and nail, risking everything they had for a selfless cause, nothing was ever straightforward. Horses were kelpies, rocks were magic, shipwrecks washed them up at feasts on the other side of the world.

They were touched in a way that at times he admired and at times he resented. And of course, he'd gone and fallen in love with the most fantastical one of all. The fairytale princess who'd worked on a fishing trawler and looked like she ought to have been born with angel wings.

And now this...

"Tell me about them."

He frowned in a way he hoped was thoughtful, trying to ignore the way his heart was still pounding in his chest. He'd thought she was dead. Plain and simple. Floating pale and frozen in the icy water, she'd looked dead. He was reeling. He'd been sure the vampire would kill him as well.

"They started not long after we left the castle..."

Evie shot him a sideways look, wondering how much to say. Thus far, she'd kept almost everything to herself. The only one she'd come close to telling was Evianna, and there was a good chance the ancient witch would have forgotten the entire confession by lunch.

But Seth was different. In a lot of ways, he was easier. He didn't come from the same world as the rest of them. He didn't share their history. He was able to be objective and fair. Yet despite all the tragedy life had thrown at him, he was unshakably optimistic. She needed both sides now.

"Mostly they're in the water," she said quietly. "There are voices in the water, bones and death. Sometimes I'm with them, sometimes I'm looking down at them. Sometimes I'm not alone."

She pulled in a shaking breath, staring down at her hands.

"Sometimes there's a dragon—bigger than any I've ever seen. He's laughing, mocking me, telling me we're too late, we're doing something wrong. Last night, I dreamt of my father."

Her voice hitched and a pair of tears slid down her face.

"That's why I froze up back there. I think a part of me was trying to remember. No matter how hard I try to figure it out, it's like we're in this puzzle. And there's always some missing piece." She peered up at him. "Does that make any sense?"

He paused a moment, then smiled sadly. "Not really."

She laughed in spite of herself, tucking her hair behind her ears. Leave it to a shifter to tell her the truth. Even when she'd almost drowned. Even when the fate of the world was at stake.

"But not much of this *has* made sense," he continued suddenly. "We tried to sail west and were thrown halfway across the world. We tried to reach the coast and ended up in an enchanted swamp. And if you're looking for rationality, I'll remind you...we're dealing with a prophecy."

She laughed again, hair spilling down her shoulders.

They were still naked, having left their clothes several mountains behind. But oddly enough, she didn't really notice. Neither was looking at the other. It felt as natural as could be.

"Everly..." His voice was quiet and serious. "Why do you think you're going to die?"

It would have been easy to write it off as nonsense, or trauma, or simple bad dreams. But as light as his new friends could be, there was a weight to the things they believed.

If she was troubled, he'd be troubled as well.

She froze like he'd slapped her, then pulled in a shuddering breath.

"Because I'm the only one having the dreams," she whispered. "I'm the only one who saw the witch, the one who was chosen to receive the prophecy. 'Three shall set out, though three shall not return.'" She shook her head, having chanted the words a thousand times before. "And that's not the worst part. You know how it ends, Seth? 'Peace will prevail, if the dragon can fly.'"

She jabbed a finger into her chest.

"I'm the dragon. *Me*. I'm the one who started this whole mess. *Me*. If the fates have written that one of us will have to make the final sacrifice, who do you think it's going to be?"

There was a long silence.

"...I'm hoping Ellanden."

She stared at him a moment, then burst into hysterical laughter. The kind peppered with sporadic tears. The kind that only got worse as he leaned down to catch her eye.

"I used to kill people for a living, Everly. We could make it look accidental."

She shook even harder, burying her head in her knees.

"What is *wrong* with you?" she demanded, trying to get a hold of herself. "I tell you this horribly serious thing, and you just—"

"You didn't tell me anything. You don't know it for sure."

The laughter stopped abruptly as she looked into his eyes.

"You don't know it for sure," he said again, even quieter this time. "You don't know if any of those things mean that you're going to die."

A sweet sentiment, but in her opinion it was incredibly naïve. It must have shown on her face because he let out a sigh, raking his fingers through wet hair.

"I'll admit...it doesn't look good," he confessed. "But aren't you always saying how tricky these things are? How nothing is ever as it seems? You *don't* know for sure." He hesitated, wary to overstep. "Either way...you should tell the others."

"No." She shook her head defiantly. "I can't."

"Evie—"

"They'll do something stupid, try to make it be about themselves." She shuddered just imagining it. "Ellanden's already far too reckless for his own good. And Asher...I can't tell them."

He looked at her appraisingly. "You don't *want* to tell them. You want it to be you."

"I don't," she replied honestly. "I don't want it to be me. But I don't want it to be my two best friends, either. And if it has to be someone..." She bowed her head, overcome by it all. "Anyway, I've been having these dreams."

The conversation fizzled out as they sat in silence, staring at the river. The air was crisp, and both were still drenched from head to toe—both had yet to realize they were shivering.

After a few minutes, the princess cast him a secret glance.

There were a lot of things they weren't saying, chief among them being how he'd probably just saved her life. She had no delusions that she would have been able to get herself out of that water. As it stood, she felt like she'd already been down there just a shade too long.

You need to thank him. We all need to stop sweeping these things under the rug.

"Seth..." She trailed off in surprise, seeing the jagged bite carved into his shoulder. "What the heck happened to you?"

He glanced down, then gave her a disbelieving stare. "You *bit* me."

Even as her mouth opened to deny it, a fleeting memory flashed back. The two of them running through the woods, her wicked delight as she nipped at him and raced forward.

...oh yeah.

"You should be more careful."

He threw back his head with a sparkling laugh.

"Oh—*my* bad!"

"You should be more careful when you choose your friends," she clarified, gesturing with mock sympathy to his shoulder. "Some of them might bite you."

He turned back to the water, shaking his head with a smile. "I'll keep that in mind."

With his attention on the river, her eyes drifted freely over him.

He really was impossibly handsome. With a flawless body, staggering eyes, and the kind of face that made her wonder why the girls of his village hadn't laid claim to him long ago. Yet in spite of it all, he was humble. He was kind. Genuine, considerate, and kind. The type of man who'd shove her playfully off a cliff, then read his little sister bedtime stories beside the light of a dying fire.

Despite the cosmic improbability...he was a *perfect* match for Cosette.

"So you're Belarian," she began conversationally. "You didn't tell me that."

He flashed a quick grin.

"No, I decided my life might be easier if I didn't." He threw her a swift look. "But I'm a shifter, you didn't think…?"

She shrugged, twirling a piece of grass in her fingers. "Not all shifters are from the same place. We have some in the High Kingdom as well."

He picked a piece for himself. "At any rate, there isn't that much jurisdiction here. At least not for a few years. I haven't thought of myself as Belarian in a long…" He trailed into silence, then looked back with a sudden smile. "When I was little, I wanted to join the Belarian Guard."

Evie glanced up with interest. "Yeah?"

He nodded, staring out over the river. "We grew up with stories about your father—the greatest wolf who ever lived." His eyes lit up with a faint smile. "There wasn't a child in my village who didn't want to move to the capital, join the infantry. We'd race around the forest for hours, waging battles, pretending to be Dylan Hale."

She warmed with a smile, but it stilled upon her face.

"I can't believe he left," she whispered. "I just…I can't believe he would do that."

Seth's eyes flashed to her face before returning quickly to the river. The princess had been asleep for ten years. He and those children had said those same words themselves many times.

They'd stopped saying them many years ago.

"That run we did this morning…it was incredible." Her eyes glowed at the memory before cooling just as fast. "I should have been doing it with him."

Seth visibly stiffened, as if there were several choice things he wanted to say. But after a moment of consideration, he settled for a simple reply. "One day soon…you will."

She threw him a look, eyes thick with tears.

He wasn't saying it to comfort her. But it was a comfort all the same. Perhaps because he so clearly meant it. There was no hint of a lie anywhere on his face.

She didn't say anything. She just nodded.

"Come on—let's head back." He stood up gracefully, offering her a hand. "The others will be awake by now. It's already coming on midday."

She nodded again and took his hand, pushing lightly to her feet. At a glance it would be a long journey back to the village on foot, but wouldn't take more than a half-hour as a wolf.

Already her body was humming with anticipation, ready to make the shift.

"Hey," she caught his arm, feeling abruptly shy, "thanks for pulling me out of there."

They glanced at the rushing water before he nodded—trying not to remember the feeling of icy terror when he dove in. They stretched their arms in preparation, bouncing a little on the balls of their feet. But a second before they could make the shift, he turned to her suddenly.

"You want to thank me...don't tell your boyfriend I pushed you off a cliff."

THE TWO SHIFTERS MADE even better time on the way back to the village, stretching out their legs and racing to the top of every peak. It wasn't the same as running with the pack, but in a way it was even more exhilarating. They could be wilder, less uniform. Leaping off trees, tumbling down ravines, and losing themselves in other adolescent acts of frivolity before coming to a sudden stop.

Evie tilted her head to the side as the sounds of the forest gave way to something else. A rustle of fabric, the clink of a hammer. The noise of the village echoing softly through the trees.

She threw Seth a confirming look, then shifted back quickly. A second before he could do the same, she threw out a quick hand—running it shamelessly over his glossy brown fur. He was still staring incredulously when he transformed a moment later, one hand lifted halfway to his hair.

"Sorry. You looked really soft."

He snorted and moved forward, stopping again when she grabbed his arm.

"What about our clothes?" she demanded.

"They're in the village."

Her eyes darted nervously through the trees. "So how are we supposed to get them?"

"We're going to walk *into* the village." He extracted his arm and began pacing through the trees. "It's a complicated formula. Try to keep up."

"Seth."

She raced around in front, feeling overwhelmed with panic. It was one thing do strip down amidst a bunch of other wolves who were all doing the same. It was quite another to stroll, perfectly naked, into the middle of town. His little sisters were there. Her friends would be watching.

"Can't you just..." She cocked her head pointedly. "...you know."

He looked down with a bemused smile. "What?"

Don't make me say it.

She gritted her teeth, well aware that threats and profanities would act against her cause.

"You know these people, I don't. Can't you just...grab my stuff and bring it back?"

"Shameless!" he laughed, dark braids swinging around his face. "You know what—you're right. You don't know these people. But my *mother's* in that village. So who should go in first?"

...you?

"Come on," she whined, pushing him towards the tree-line. "You don't care about any of that—you're a shifter! You were about to do it anyway, just two seconds before."

"That's before I found out what a pathetic little coward you are."

She jutted up her chin. "Coward? I jumped off a *cliff*."

He rolled his eyes. "I pushed you off the cliff. You refused to go on your own."

She lit up with sudden inspiration.

"That's right...you pushed me off a cliff." With a wicked smile, she folded her arms across her chest. "You pushed me off a cliff. And I'm dating a vampire."

There was a moment of silence.

Then he turned on his heel. "...I'll be right back."

JUST FIVE MINUTES LATER he returned, fully dressed, carrying a bundle of clothes with him. He tossed them at the princess with no warning, flashing a grin when they struck her in the face.

"*Everyone* saw me," he complained theatrically. "*Everyone* laughed."

She tugged the dress over her head with a smile.

"Well, you're funny to look at. I often laugh myself."

When she emerged a moment later, the teasing was finished and he gallantly offered out his arm. She accepted rather daintily, and together they started walking through the trees.

"So I have a question..." she began slowly, glancing from the corner of her eye. "Are you going to tell your mother what happened?"

His arm tensed beneath hers.

For a few seconds, it was quiet. But when he answered it sounded strangely scripted, as if he'd been saying it over and over to himself.

"Jack is her brother," he said softly. "After my father died, she trusted him to take care of things. Something like this would break her heart."

Exactly. Something like this.

"I'm not indifferent to that...but this wasn't some casual betrayal," she answered carefully, watching him all the while. "By your own uncle's estimation, you should have died in that arena. If Cosette hadn't freed you, it's likely you would have been dead already. Your mother's still waiting for him to come back, like everything is fine. Doesn't she deserve to know?"

It was *absolutely* over the line. It was *absolutely* none of her business. But the two had spent the entire morning together. He'd dragged her naked from an alpine stream. Point being, lines blurred.

"People like my uncle..." He trailed off and started again. "The thing is...people like my uncle...they took what work came their way."

A generous way of saying it. But as they cleared the trees and entered the village, it seemed that a little generosity was required.

The friends had been so utterly depleted by the time they wandered into the village, that salient details had blended together and vague generalities had ruled the day.

The princess had surmised the village was poor.

It was *very* poor.

People weren't just hungry—they were gaunt. If Seth's experience had been anything like the others', the Red Hand would have had to fatten him up a bit before placing a sword in his hand. The schoolhouse wasn't the only building that was abandoned. Pails came back from the well half-empty.

But the place was not reflected in the people.

Never in her life had Evie seen such happy, welcoming people.

"Your home...it's really great."

Seth glanced at her in surprise, then turned away with a smile. "Yeah, it is."

Apparently, they weren't the only ones to think so. The others had taken advantage of their absence to ingratiate themselves with the village. And from the looks of things, they were doing an amazing job. Cosette and Ellanden were playing with the children, while Freya was chatting with Seth's mother by one of the outdoor fires. Even Asher had worked past his fear of ostracization and was sitting with the village elders, nodding thoughtfully as one of them jabbed their finger at a book.

Evie watched them with a smile, stretching up to murmur in Seth's ear. "Do you think they know what he is?"

It was a fair question. For as long as she could remember, the princess had travelled with the vampire around the five kingdoms. He'd never received a welcome quite so warm as this.

Even the Kreo tried to drown him before making him dinner.

"What do you mean?" Seth asked curiously.

She flashed him a look. "Do they know he's a vampire?"

His mouth fell open in shock. "Asher's a *vampire*?! Why didn't you tell me!"

A group of passing shifters glanced over their shoulders as she smacked him with a grin.

"You know, if you really are one of my subjects, I'm definitely having you executed the second this doomsday mission is done. Death by slapping. It'll take ages. I'll participate myself."

He laughed carelessly. "Don't be silly, Your Highness. If the fates have their way, you'll be dead long before then."

She looked at him in shock.

"...too soon?"

Yeah.

He walked away whistling and she couldn't help but laugh. *Wolves.* Instead of interrupting her boyfriend's rare bonding with the townsfolk, she headed over to Freya instead.

The girl was standing by herself now, tilting her head as she stared contemplatively at a pile of logs. At some point in the night it had apparently rained, and aside from a few precarious flames most of the courtyard blazes had yet to materialize. The witch considered this one for a moment, lifted her hands with a flourish, then doused the entire thing in a spray of magical light. There was a wild hissing sound, followed by a spattering of applause. A second later, the fire sprang to life.

The princess stepped back in surprise—surprise that tripled when she glanced back at the villagers, all of whom had already returned to whatever they were doing before. As a rule, shifters didn't take too kindly to other forms of magic. Even less so to a pyromaniac witch. But very few of those social prejudices seemed to have made it so far into the mountains. Case in point: Asher was now openly laughing with the gaggle of old men up on the porch.

"Nice work." She warmed her hands above the dancing flames, not realizing how cold she was until that very moment. "You should take those tricks on the road. Try to make some coin."

Freya shrugged in a rare moment of modesty. "Royalty is better suited to turning tricks for coin. And anyway, your fire is much more impressive than mine."

The princess laughed shortly. "Oh, I don't know about that."

Never would she be able to forget how the young witch stood fearlessly in front of a horde of vampires, ripples of iridescent light shimmering up and down her arms. She was a vision. Lovely but terrifying all at the same time. Even the wraithlike immortals stepped back at the sight.

The princess had never seen anything like it. Not even that day on the beach.

Perhaps I just need to find the right motivation...

As if reading her thoughts, Freya's eyes shot instantly across the courtyard to Ellanden before clouding moodily and returning to the flames. "Yeah, well...that was a mistake."

Evie's eyebrows shot into her hair.

"A mistake?" she repeated, astonished the girl would even acknowledge her not-so-secret infatuation let alone give up the chase. "What do you mean?"

A dusting of honey-colored bangs swept into Freya's eyes, momentarily hiding them from view. When she tossed them back once again, she was a different person.

"Cosette's right," she said curtly. "It was a silly childhood crush. Don't know why I was obsessing over it. Nothing more to it than that."

Evie's voice softened gently. "Freya—"

"At any rate, there's plenty to do right here." She lifted her hands, moving swiftly to the next pile of logs. "Like right now, I'm making myself useful by setting things on fire."

Cosette's right. We need to keep an eye on you.

"Okay, can I just say something?" The princess trailed after her, watching as streams of liquid light flew from her palms. "First of all, I love Cosette to pieces but I wouldn't take any advice from her when it comes to matters of the heart." Her eyes drifted to where the lovely fae was still playing with the children, oblivious to the handsome shifter tracking every move with his eyes. "And I know you, Freya. The way you feel for him...it *isn't* nothing."

The witch kept her eyes on the fire, but her shoulders fell with a defeated sigh.

"He thinks I'm a child," she said softly. "He thinks I'm six years old. And I can't blame him for that. We joke about it all the time, but that was literally a few *weeks* ago to you guys. In his mind, he was carrying me on his shoulders and reading me bedtime stories a few weeks ago." She glanced behind her before returning to the fire. "That's probably why he's so against Cosette and Seth."

Evie stepped in front of her, eyes stinging with the heat of the blaze.

"I have no idea why he's so against Cosette and Seth," she admitted, though she had a sneaking suspicion it harkened back to their days in the nursery—when he refused to let anyone else play with his toys. "But this isn't some frivolous crush. And I can prove it."

Freya rolled her eyes sarcastically. "You can prove it?"

"I know what happened the night of the shipwreck," the princess said bluntly. "I saw the two of you in the water, after the storm threw us into the sea."

In a venom-induced haze in the middle of the Kreo jungle, the vision had come to her clear as day. The prince had been tangled in rope, unable to free himself, vanishing quickly into the murky depths. But the witch found him, stayed with him, kissed air into his lungs.

Freya was stunned, unable to speak.

"You saved him," Evie finished quietly. "That isn't *nothing*, Freya. You saved his life—"

"Except I didn't," the witch interrupted with sudden fierceness. "I tried to save him...and I couldn't. He's the one who saves people. I basically sentenced him to die!"

"You didn't sentence him to anything," Evie argued. "He was already going to die. And you stayed with him. He was going to die alone...but you stayed."

There was a heavy pause before the witch turned away.

"He doesn't remember that that."

"Then make him remember," Evie insisted. "Tell him what happened."

"It doesn't matter."

"Frey—"

"He doesn't *like* me, Everly," she snapped. "Is that simple enough for you? I can't trick him into it by failing to save his life—totally endearing, by the way. He just doesn't like me."

The princess stared at her a moment, then shook her head. "...I'm not sure about that."

No, there had been nothing overt. And for a flirtatious person like Ellanden, that alone might have been enough to throw someone off his tracks. But he looked after the witch more tenderly than the others, watching over her even when she slept. He'd dismissed the shifter who'd tried to proposition her at the Kreo dance. When Evie had mentioned she might have feelings for him, he hadn't looked inconvenienced or evasive—he'd been genuinely surprised.

Toys in the nursery. He wanted the best ones for himself.

Freya's eyes shot up, filled with an emotion she wasn't quick enough to hide. "He thinks I'm a child—"

"The Fae think *everyone* are children. You need to stake your claim." The witch laughed at this.

"Stake my claim?" Her eyes drifted once more over the field, staring tentatively before she laughed suddenly once again. "I'm too late."

Evie followed her gaze, grinning from ear to ear.

News had apparently gotten out that there was a little more to their strange visitors than met the eye. As it stood playtime had ended and both fae were kneeling on the ground, swarmed by a cluster of overexcited children. Some of them were whispering behind their hands, gawking openly at Cosette's ivory hair, while a little girl had stepped bravely in front of Ellanden, holding out a hand.

"...may I?"

It was a testament to how many times this had happened that the prince didn't need to ask what she meant. Instead he inclined his head with a smile, holding very still as she brushed back his hair with an absurdly serious expression and touched the tip of her finger to one of his pointed ears.

Her eyes widened with a gasp. "Does it hurt?" she whispered.

He laughed affectionately, catching her tiny wrist. "No, sweetheart. It doesn't hurt."

If it was possible, the vampire was getting even more attention.

Asher had wandered away from his geriatric book club and was lingering at the edge of the swarm, watching with amusement as his friends were accosted by the most delicate of attackers time and time again. But when they saw him standing there, the tables swiftly turned.

"And that's him! That's the one!"

In a flash, the tiny crowd shifted—enveloping the vampire as well.

He froze uncertainly, sucking in a quick breath as they grabbed him by the wrists and yanked him down to their height. It was an experience with which he was completely unfamiliar.

Vampires didn't have the same ethereal attraction of the Fae. They were predators at heart. Hypnotically bewitching predators—but predators all the same.

Animals shied away from them. Children instinctively gave them a wide berth.

But not these children.

"Feel his hands—they're so cold!"

Asher froze dead still, pale as a statue, looking like he was trapped in the world's most adorable petting zoo. He cast a panicked glance at Ellanden, but the fae only grinned—nudging a few of them closer for a better look. "He's also very fun to climb," he whispered conspiratorially.

The same little girl who'd touched Ellanden's ears ventured towards the front of the group, cocking her head with a pair of appraising eyes. "Are you really a vampire?"

Her voice softened him with a smile.

"Would that be so terrible?" he answered softly.

She considered a moment.

"No...I suppose not." She grinned shyly in return, swishing her dress. Then her eyes lit with sudden excitement. "May I see your fangs?"

Seth threw a quick look across the courtyard, and Asher shook his head with a smile.

"Maybe some other time."

He gracefully got to his feet. The children scattered with their customary feral shrieks, off to seek out their next thrill. His eyes followed along until they rounded a corner and vanished into the woods, gentling with an expression the princess had never seen.

"I never understood why you liked them so much," he murmured to Ellanden. "Children, I mean. Sure, they're amusing, but I never...they're actually rather sweet."

Ellanden cast him a look of surprise. "You've always loved Cosette. Why should other children be so different?"

The vampire lifted his shoulders with a teasing grin. "I loved Cosette because someone had to. You and Evie were so horrible to her."

"He's right," Cosette said authoritatively, dusting off her dress while the others joined them in the middle of the courtyard. "You two were gone a long time. How was your run?"

The two shifters paused, then looked in opposite directions.

"Fine."

"It was fine."

Asher looked at them curiously, then tilted his head with a smile. "It's good you came back when you did. It sounds like the others are gearing up for a hunt—"

A quiet profanity echoed behind them as Charlotte stepped out of the cabin, pouring an overflowing bucket into the garden bed nearby. Seth hurried towards her without a moment's pause, his brow creased with concern. The others trailed discreetly a few steps behind.

"What happened?" he asked as soon as he was within earshot.

She glanced up in surprise, then was quick to shake her head.

"Oh, nothing. Sorry." Her head tilted back towards the cabin. "Just this roof. It rained last night and flooded part of your sisters' bedroom."

He glanced up in alarm, squinting slightly in the sun.

"I can fix that for you," he said immediately, pulling off his cloak and kneeling down to unlace his shoes. "How long has it been going on?"

A flash of emotion shot across her face, but she cleared it with a smile. "Don't worry about it, honey. Keep your shoes on."

He ignored her, tossing his boots onto the grass.

"Where's Darren?" he asked instead. "Isn't he supposed to take care of these sorts of things when the pack is away?"

There was that strange look again. The princess watched her curiously.

"It's *fine*." Charlotte caught his hands, forcing them still. "If you want, you can take a look at it later. For now, you need to hunt. The village is dining together tonight."

His face lightened in surprise. "Why?"

She stared a moment, then her lips crooked up in a smile. "To welcome you home."

Chapter 11

It wasn't a feast. You couldn't call it that. It was too small to be a feast. It was too cold outside, with too little food, even though the wolves had spent the better part of the day hunting.

But it was a feast unlike any the princess had ever seen.

It was like slipping into someone else's family, if only for a night. People weren't just eating their dinner, they were bickering over recipes. People weren't just listening to the music, they were calling out requests. Stories were the real currency of the evening. Someone was always telling one, someone else was always correcting them. The whole affair couldn't last five minutes without the entire village bursting into spontaneous laughter at some ancient joke.

In a strange way, it reminded Evie very strongly of the huge 'family dinners' she used to have back at the castle with her parents and all of their friends. They were just as lively and just as unruly.

Despite having significantly fewer people than the village, they drank just as much wine.

I miss this, she thought dreamily, stretching her legs on the ground. *I want to have this again.*

Ellanden was sitting beside her, flushed and smiling, leaning back against a fallen tree. His head nodded gently in time with the music, and every so often he'd reach down and massage his leg.

The princess bit back a grin. "How are you feeling?"

Despite his inconvenient tendency to 'stay human', the fae had opted to go with the pack as they set off into the mountains to hunt. The result had been...interesting.

He flashed her a quick look, then bowed his head with a smile.

"I'm exhausted," he admitted, rubbing his leg once again. "Seriously, Evie—I don't know what I was thinking. The next time I suggest such a thing, punch me in the face."

There was a quiet murmur of laughter from a few shifters around them, while Seth's mother reached down to give his shoulder a comforting squeeze.

"Everyone said you did well," she said reassuringly. "They were amazed you kept pace."

"Yes, but he almost killed himself in the process," Asher said fondly. "Should have just let me come along, too. I could have carried you back down the mountain."

Evie poked the fae in the side. "Or you could just stop being so pathetic."

"Have you ever tried running alongside a wolf?" he demanded. "As a *human*? I was the only person there with two legs."

Another burst of laughter and Evie's gaze drifted with lazy contentment around the fire.

While the rest of them were forgoing the party, sipping hot mugs of chicory in a state of recline, Cosette was right there in the thick of it. Her hair had been braided by children's hands, strung up and styled like the rest of the pack, and she was dancing with the rest of them as a banjo and penny-whistle sang out in front of the fire. Every so often, one of the children would howl with their face pointed up at the moon. The rest of them would shriek with delight before joining in.

After a few rounds of watching them, the Fae princess joined in herself.

Evie glanced a few seats down, and sure enough Seth was watching from his place at the table, looking as though he'd stepped into a dream. His eyes twinkled as they followed every move, clapping along with the others. But for one of the first times, Cosette was watching him back. Every minute or so she'd glance over her shoulder, catching his gaze with an enchanting smile. He blushed a little at the spectacle, rolling his eyes like it was all some big joke. But there was unmistakable pride in where he'd come from, in the people who'd made him who he was.

Charlotte glanced twice between them, reading the situation as only a mother could. After a few minutes she nudged him gently, eyes dancing with amusement as he startled in surprise.

"She's very pretty," she said with a coaxing smile. "How did you two meet?"

He froze a split second, then forced a quick smile of his own. "I, uh...borrowed her necklace."

Evie snorted into her drink.

That's one way of putting it.

"Her necklace?"

Charlotte raised her eyebrows with an expression very reminiscent of her son. When he wouldn't give her anything further, she went right to the source.

"Cosette?" she called innocently.

Seth whitened in panic. "Mom, don't—"

The lovely fae glanced towards the tables in surprise.

"Come here a moment, dear." She stood up gracefully, lifting a handful of plates. "I could use some help with these."

The shifter grabbed a handful of her dress. "If you love me...sit back down."

She stroked his cheek with a smile. "It's too late, darling. She's heading over here already." Her eyes twinkled in the dark. "But I'm sure you have nothing to worry about. After all, you simply borrowed her necklace."

Before he could do anything to stop it the two women joined each other at the table and picked up what they could carry, heading off together towards the well.

Seth stared after them, looking like he'd swallowed a knife.

"Well, that's one way to do it," Ellanden said cheerfully.

"...what?"

"Stop this fledgling relationship before it can get off the ground." He clinked his glass against Evie's with a self-satisfied smile. "We don't give our mothers enough credit."

The shifter blanched, but could think of nothing to say.

Evie took the rest of her drink and poured it onto the fae's leg.

For the next hour or so, the celebration continued on in fine spirits, finally fizzling suddenly into the dark. The children were put to bed, stronger alcohol was brought forth—a homemade liquor that made Evie's head spin just to sniff it—and the musicians put down their instruments, sitting down among the rest of them as conversations carried on and drifted into the night.

Cosette and Charlotte had returned not long before. It was hard to interpret the looks on their faces, neither one of them saying a single word. But the fae surprised everyone by darting in and giving her a quick hug before settling herself quickly on the opposite side of the fire.

For once, Seth wasn't watching. His eyes were on something else.

"Where is everyone?" he murmured to no one in particular.

There was a hitch in Charlotte's breathing before she sank into the chair by his side.

"So Asher," she began with forced cheer, "were they able to find you something—"

"Darren, Silas, Lukas..." Seth's gaze roved over the people gathered by the fire, noticing gaps in the circle for the first time. When he made it once around, he glanced back at his mother. "Is there another hunting party?" he asked, unable to think of another explanation. "Did Harrison take a group of people farther west—"

"Finish your drink," she interrupted casually. When his face tensed in alarm she smoothed back his hair, tempering it with a motherly smile. "You look tired, honey. Don't worry about all that right now—"

"What's there to worry about?" he interrupted sharply, pulling away from her hand. Their eyes locked for a moment. "Mom...why is the schoolhouse shut down?"

She abruptly went pale, clutching the folds of her dress. The people sitting around them quieted as well, casting each other quick looks before struggling to pick up where they'd left off.

"Seth, this isn't the time—"

"Why didn't Darren fix your roof?" he pressed. "We have an arrangement for that sort of thing. Why is there a leak in the girls' bedroom?"

"Please, let's not—"

"*Mom.*"

She let out a quiet sigh, and it felt as though the celebration stopped and the eyes of the entire village were on them. Faces were riddled with worry and fear, but on Charlotte's face there was nothing but a quiet steadiness. And a cold dread as to what her headstrong son would do next.

"They were taken."

Seth pulled in a sharp breath, running through a catalogue of faces in his mind.

"Taken? By who?"

No one answered. It looked like no one *could* answer.

He pushed to his feet, glaring at the crowd.

"*Taken by who?*"

"SLAVERS!"

The shifter shouted the word for the hundredth time, pacing furiously back and forth. After the shocking revelation in the village the friends had taken the initiative to walk him to the forest, where he could rant and rave without frightening the locals. He'd done so in spades. Several trees were already splintered across the ground as collateral.

"I mean, can you believe it?!" he cried. "Can you bloody believe it?!"

The friends stood in silence, watching with quiet, worried eyes.

"My uncle was supposed to be sending back money, to be providing some degree of protection. The *entire* reason I went with him was so that my family—" He cut himself short, eyes darkening with the blackest kind of hate. "When I was there, he'd send people back all the time to check on things. Keeping tabs on the village—that's what he'd call it. For all I know they were just scouting potential victims, sending the information along to the fort!"

At last, they were getting somewhere. A new word had entered the conversation.

"The fort?" Ellanden repeated quietly.

"It's about fifty miles north of here, nestled in a crest of mountains." Seth's eyes flashed with rage. "When we were younger, it used to be a stop for merchants. Now, I guess it's used for this."

Evie stared in nervous silence.

It was the most she'd heard him talk. Ever. The man was cheerful and friendly, but he'd settled into a quieter role in their group. Listening instead of speaking, feeling out the dynamic as he learned everything he could about his new friends. Big speeches like this weren't his style.

Neither was the anger he made no attempt to control.

"How do you..." she paused, not wanting to escalate things, "how do you know it was your uncle? There are lots of slavers around these parts. Maybe it had nothing to do with—"

"It had EVERYTHING to do with him!"

Another sapling crashed to the ground, torn by the shifter's bare hand.

"Even if he didn't sell them directly, it was his fault. HE was supposed to be here. HE was supposed to protect them." He stopped suddenly, like he was catching his breath. "And we all know he doesn't have a problem betraying his own blood."

A ringing silence fell over the forest, pounding in their ears.

Seth never talked about the time he'd spent enslaved in Tarnaq, but it was never far from his mind. Sometimes as they were walking through the forest, his eyes would darken suddenly and a hand would drift to his neck. Other times he would tremble in his sleep, trapped once more in that arena, staring down nightmares and demons as the crowd screamed for blood.

"That fort is heavily guarded," he murmured to himself, turning slightly to stare at a particular spot between the peaks. "Now that it's run by slavers, I imagine it's even worse." He shook his head slightly, clenching his teeth. "You know, when we were kids we used to pretend that we lived there. We *wished* that we lived there. Because it was protected. Because once you were inside you knew you were safe."

Asher took a step forward, radiating that eternal calm.

"How is it protected?" he asked softly. "Besides the guards."

Seth let out a sigh, raking his fingers back through his hair.

"Walls are too high for climbing, too thick for a battering ram. They're pure stone to shield against fire, and the door is protected by a drawbridge over a moat. There is no way to get inside."

He stood there a second longer, then began striding swiftly through the trees.

"Where are you going?" Cosette cried.

"I'm going to get inside."

The friends froze a moment, then took off after him.

It wasn't easy to follow him. Shifters moved with a natural ease, and despite their own gifts he'd grown up in these woods. For a terrifying second amidst the mad scramble, they actually lost him. Then the princess spotted a dark head of hair moving through the trees.

"Wait a second," she panted. "Just think about this—"

"There's no time," he answered curtly, eyes on the trail. "For all I know, they've already been sold to a buyer. I need to get there. *Now*."

And then what?

The man was armed with only a blunt sword he'd found in his childhood bedroom. His steps were already unsteady from the liquor at the feast. But none of that mattered. The princess highly doubted he'd use a blade, and she highly doubted he'd enter the fortress on his own two feet.

The second he was within sight of the walls she fully expected him to shift and charge straight towards it, tearing the thing apart with his claws.

...and they'll kill him.

"You can't go!"

"Watch me—"

"You *can't*. It's too much to do by yourself." He paused suddenly and she pressed her advantage. "The only thing you'll accomplish is getting yourself killed. Think of your mother. Think of your sisters. You can't do something like that to them. You need to calm down."

Cosette slipped past her, staring into his eyes.

"Please listen to her. One man could never make it into a fortress. It doesn't matter if you come as a wolf or not—if there are any archers, they'll shoot you on sight."

Evie stood squarely behind her, muscles tensed in case he tried to run.

"Just take a breath. Go back to the village. We can talk to your mother and find out—"

"You're right."

The princess stopped short.

"...I am?"

He nodded slowly, eyes glowing with the hint of a plan.

"You're right...I can't do it by myself."

Another silence fell over the clearing as he lifted his gaze to the rest of them.

Seven hells.

APPROVAL

"I've never asked for anything," he said softly, looking at each of them in turn. "I've followed you everywhere, risked everything you needed, done anything you thought was best. I've never asked for anything...but I'm asking for this. I know what it means...and I'm asking."

No one answered. It was as if the entire clearing had turned to stone.

On the one hand, they were already on board. Slavery was despicable. They'd recently dined with the latest victims of its crimes and, truth be told, Seth didn't need a good reason to demand their allegiance. They'd risk a lot more than he was asking, just to satisfy a casual whim.

But the actual *thing* he was asking made them pause.

Fortresses were conquered with armies. Entire battalions of soldiers. Ones with armor and weapons and supplies. They were not taken down by a handful of teenagers with nothing but a handful of blades and the power of righteousness on their side.

Seth would be killed if he went alone. But all of them would surely be killed if they went together. It would just take longer for the fort to collect the bodies, that's all.

And there was that matter of the prophecy. Shouldn't they be heading west?

"Your *Highness*."

Evie's head snapped up in surprise. It was the first time he'd called her such a thing with any degree of sincerity, but he couldn't be more serious about it now. Their eyes met, and in a flash she was reminded of their alpine run that morning. Streaking through the forest, at the head of the pack.

MY pack. These are MY people.
Taken for slaves.

"I'll go with you."

She surprised them all by saying it, but none more than herself. Seth's eyes gleamed as he gave her a little nod. But she was only the first. There were several more to go.

"Asher?"

An interesting choice. But the vampire wasn't looking at the shifter. He was looking at his girlfriend, eyes fixed on the side of her face. After a few seconds he nodded with a soft affirmation.

"Yes, all right."

There was a sudden crunching of leaves as Freya marched towards the shifter, throwing a casual arm around his neck. "Well, you already know I'm on board. Then again, I *am* the bravest..."

He chuckled quietly, lifting his gaze to the beautiful girl standing in the trees.

"Cosette?"

She looked at him calmly, her face betraying not an iota of emotion. Unless they touched on precisely the right subject, fae weren't often moved by speeches or platitudes. They agreed with what you were saying, or they didn't. There was very little room in which they could be convinced.

But she didn't make him wait long, and she didn't disappoint. With a little smile she crossed the distance between them, sliding her hand into his.

"I'm with you," she said simply.

Their fingers laced together and they stared deep into each other's eyes. Then he turned slowly, almost fearfully, to where her handsome cousin stood a few steps behind.

"...Landi?"

It was the first time he'd ever called him such a thing. The gesture could have almost been seen as sweet, if it wasn't infused with such an obvious dose of fear.

Ellanden stared at him a moment, then tilted his head.

"Why do you think *I'd* have a problem with it?" he asked with a little smile. "I'm apparently reckless and irresponsible. This should be right up my alley..."

Chapter 12

On paper, it was a suicide mission.

In Evie's experience, suicide missions were usually the kinds of things that should be launched into immediately, probably drunk, before anyone had a chance for second thoughts. Their own fated prophecy was a suicide mission. She liked to think she knew how these things worked.

But the fortress was different.

"There isn't any room for error," Seth said for the tenth time, jabbing a stick down at the picture he'd drawn in the dirt. "These people are known for executing prisoners. If we're going to get them out safely, we need to be precise and quick."

It had been a hard sell—convincing the shifter to come back down from the mountain. His childhood friends were chained up somewhere on the other side, and with the feel of a salcor so fresh upon his own neck, he simply couldn't fathom walking away.

But this piece of logic had done it. If they made a mistake, they'd execute a prisoner. Asher had said it first, hoping to temper the shifter's impatience. But Seth had quickly adopted it himself, chanting it like a mantra, drilling it into the others though there was no longer any need.

In the end, they'd gone back to the village. He'd apologized to his mother. He'd assured her that he'd fix the roof in the morning, that these things happened, but there wasn't anything to fear.

He'd lied.

At the moment, the friends sat on the floor of the schoolhouse—planning their early morning assault on the fortress, drawing desperate, hopeless pictures in the dust.

"I still don't know how we're going to scale the wall," he muttered, rubbing his face as they stared down at the crude drawing. "It's a perfect square, with about ten guards on every side and a giant bell in the middle that they'll ring if there's any trouble. *Ten* guards," he repeated, trying not to sound as disheartened as he felt. "How are we supposed to scale the sides in time? Before *ten* different people see us? And that's *if* we manage to cross the moat without anyone being the wiser."

Ellanden leaned forward with a frown, touching the tip of his finger to the bell.

"You're sure we don't have *any* access to a bow?" he asked yet again. "If it's even remotely functional, I can take down at least one set of guards before the others realize what's happening. If that works I can just fire around the bell, make sure the rest can't get close enough to touch it—"

"My people don't fight with bows," Seth interrupted. "There isn't anything like that in the village. And even if you kept them away from the bell, the others could just shout."

It was silent a few moments.

"What about me?" Asher asked quietly, his dark eyes catching the moonlight as he stared down at the drawing. "I could scale the walls without anyone noticing. I could take out at least half of the guards before anyone could see. As for the rest of them...what if I took Evie and Freya with me? They could spread out on either side, take down those remaining with fire."

Seth lifted his eyebrows, considering, but Cosette shook her head.

"That only accounts for the people guarding the upper perimeter. Most of the soldiers will be waiting inside. Even if you managed to subdue enough of those to tear down the gate, we'd still be outnumbered fifty to one...and they'd start executing the prisoners."

The plan was abandoned. They were back to square one.

"We could get as close as we can, then spray fire from the forest?"

"The fortress is made of stone."

"We could head back to a trading post, get some *actual* weapons and supplies."

"They would be sold in the meantime. We'd never see them again."

Back and forth they went for the better part of an hour, yielding fewer and fewer results. It might not have been pleasant, but there was a reason the slavers had chosen to make the fort their stronghold. No matter which angle you came at it, there simply wasn't a way to get inside.

After a while, they were no longer gathered around the map. They were leaning back against the abandoned desks and tables, rubbing their eyes and wracking their tired brains.

"Evie could just shift into a dragon, that would solve all our problems," Ellanden suggested caustically before shooting her a look. "Oh, I forgot...you can't."

She gave him a cold glare. "Can you even walk on that leg?"

"Guys, that isn't helping," Asher said quietly. "Come on, let's try to focus—"

"We've been looping the same ideas for hours," Ellanden countered, gesturing impatiently to the map. "It isn't a matter of focus."

"So what are you saying?" Seth challenged, more desperate than the others and with far more to lose. "That we should just give up?"

"Of course not," the fae snapped. "But wouldn't it be easier if we just waited until they were sold? We could set up camp in the forest, intercept the carriages—"

"You don't know what will happen to them in the meantime."

That brought the conversation to a momentary pause.

"No, I don't," the fae conceded softly. "And having been through it yourself, I can't imagine how this must feel to you. But the point is, if we can't infiltrate the fortress we're going to have to wait until your friends come back through the gate—"

"And then what?" the shifter demanded, losing all grip on his temper. He was choosing a dangerous opponent, but in the heat of the moment he didn't seem to care. "They're not all going to the same place. For all we know, some of them could be staying indefinitely at the fort."

"The second we attacked the first carriage, they'd send reinforcements," Evie added, staring wearily at the floor. "They'd hole up in the fort and wouldn't risk moving anyone again until they'd found us. With our luck, they'd go back to the village to replenish their supply—"

Seth pushed angrily to his feet, unable to hear anymore.

"In that case, what do you suggest?" Ellanden asked with strained patience. "I'm not trying to upset you, I'm only saying that we're running out of moves—"

"Do you still have the salcor?" Freya asked suddenly, turning to Cosette.

The fae looked up in surprise, tearing her eyes from the window.

"Actually—yes." She lifted the hem of her dress to show a delicate silver chin wrapped around her ankle. "I was wearing it in the shipwreck, and the vampires and Kreo didn't think to check. Turns out it's not so easy to lose. But what good would it do?"

The witch's eyes danced with mischief as a slow smile spread up her face.

"I have an idea..."

"IT IS JUST SO TYPICAL...that I'd get stuck here with you."

Evie twisted her head to the side, finding herself face to face with Ellanden. Even so close, it was dark enough that he was hard to see. She felt instead, lifting her fingers to his face.

More specifically, to his eyes.

"...*ow*."

"Sorry," she breathed, retracting them at once. "Just trying to figure out where you are."

"I'm *here*," came the sarcastic reply. "Right bloody here. Keep your hands to yourself."

She bit her lip and turned away, hoping he couldn't see her smile.

For the last four hours, they'd been hiking through the forest. For the last four hours before that, they'd been breaking their backs trying to spruce the village wagon into something a little more presentable, something a little bit faster, and something a little more suited to their cause.

"There," Seth had announced when it was complete, "it's perfect."

The rest of the friends leaned over slowly, staring into the darkness.

It was a smuggler's compartment. At least it was meant to be. In reality, it was a twelve-inch trough hidden in the bottom of the wagon. By removing two nails a plank in the floor came loose, allowing a person to slip unseen underneath. Put the plank back on top, and no one was the wiser.

One person could fit relatively comfortably. Two would be almost impossible to manage. It also had to be said it had looked incredibly difficult to breathe in...

After a few seconds, Ellanden lifted his head.

"Again—this looks *exactly* like a coffin."

The others snorted with laugher. This time it was easy to see the resemblance, much easier than with the boat. Seth looked down himself, noticing it for the first time before flashing a smile.

"What can I say?" he asked innocently. "When I think of places I'd like to put you..."

"It's better than riding beneath the wagon," Freya inserted helpfully. "At least you're not strapped with rope to the wrong side."

That had been the first plan. This had been the second.

The fae hadn't been impressed with either.

"Why can't Seth and I switch roles?" he complained. "Surely I proved myself back on the beach. And if things start to go south, the man is absolute rubbish in a fight."

The shifter pulled his knife, giving it an expert twirl.

Asher was quick to intercede.

"That's all perfectly true," he answered in the voice one might use to coddle a child, "but you're too much of a threat. Everyone knows the Fae are powerful. We don't want you to put them on guard. But Seth...who would suspect him? The man's a simpleton, can hardly carry a blade."

There was a pointed silence. Then Seth dropped the knife.

"See?" Asher finished with a smile. "You'll be our secret weapon."

The fae looked at him coldly, unmoved by the theatrics. "Do you honestly think that's going to work?"

Asher smiled sweetly, holding up the plank. "I think, whether it does or not, you're getting into that hole."

And so it was...

It was a tight squeeze, a *very* tight squeeze, but Evie and Ellanden had forced themselves down into the little compartment. Holding their breaths and turning their faces as the plank was hammered back into place on the other side. Hammered *loosely*—that part was important.

"Would you stop messing with it?" Evie asked, watching as the fae wedged his fingers against the nail, giving it an experimental push. "It's going to open. We've already tried."

He nodded and lowered his arm back to his side. A second later he was at it again.

She closed her eyes with a sigh. "You are impossible..."

In the beginning, they'd been afraid to talk. What if someone else could hear them? What if there were spies in the woods, or they were getting closer to the fortress than they'd thought?

After about five minutes of bumping up and down on the unpaved road, they no longer cared.

Claustrophobic, she thought to herself. *I never knew I was claustrophobic.*

Oddly enough, it made her want to get closer.

"Landi," she whispered, inching her way to his side, "do you think we should have a signal?"

There wasn't far to go. After just a split second, scooting painfully to the left, she was already pressed right up against him—twisting her head painfully to see his face.

It was irritated. And *very* close.

"A signal?" he repeated, trying and failing to move the other way.

"For in case this all goes terribly wrong," she clarified, keeping herself talking through sheer force of will. "The others would be able to just run away, but you and I are stuck down here. I think we should probably have some kind of signal."

The fae sighed quietly, staring through the slats in the wood. Every now and then his face would flash with a burst of fading sunlight, but for the most part things were shadowy black.

"And what would this signal imply?" he quipped. "Would it tell us to run? To fight? Would it tell us to stay very quiet and hope that the nail is actually loose enough to escape?"

She thought about it for a second. "I suppose it would tell you to spirit me to safety."

He laughed quietly at that, holding himself bracingly as the cart bumped over what felt like every rut in the five kingdoms. There was no way to protect oneself. It was nearly impossible just to turn one's head. When the wheels dipped, they simply smashed their heads into the plank above them. It happened so many times, Ellanden was finally forced to ask the question.

"Is Seth the one steering?"

There was a distant chuckle, followed by two quick slaps to the cart.

The fae flinched and ground his teeth together. "When all this is finished, I'm going to bury that boy in a shallow grave."

Evie smiled happily. "I think he's great. You should go easier on him."

Ellanden rolled his eyes. "He should go...away."

"I'm serious," she continued. "He's a much better person than you are. More likeable, too. I think, if you kept an open mind, you could probably learn a lot—"

"Does Asher like this about you?" he interrupted irritably. "This constant need to force your opinions on the people around you?" He flexed his cramped legs, trying to maintain circulation. "I know the vampire is lonely, but it makes me want to wrap my hands around your throat."

"The vampire can hear you just fine," a voice echoed from somewhere above them.

Oh. Right.

She waited a second out of politeness then scooted even closer, stopping just an inch away from his face. "Does it make you nervous—being in here?"

He closed his eyes, counting backwards from ten. "I'm fine."

"Claustrophobic, I mean. Does it make you claustrophobic?"

There was a beat.

"Well, it does now."

She let out a wistful sigh, dreaming of legroom and sunshine. Truth be told, they hadn't been in the wagon all that long. They had walked most of the way from the village, helping carry the rickety wheels over the rougher parts of the road. But the second that plank was nailed into place, time ceased to matter. They might as well have been lying there a hundred years.

"I'm glad you're here with me," she murmured, running the tips of her fingers along the slats of wood. "Even if your height has become an immediate problem. I'm glad it's not just me alone."

He was stayed quiet for a moment, then turned towards her. "I could kiss you."

She lit up with a smile, feeling profoundly touched. "Really? I thought you'd be mad—"

"No, I mean I could *actually* kiss you. By accident." He kicked at her legs. "Go back to your own side. You're crowding me."

That was the last of the talking.

WHAT FELT LIKE YEARS later, the little wagon finally rolled to a stop. The princess knew it for sure because there'd been a sudden lurching motion and her head smashed into the ceiling. There was some quiet talking, a gentle creaking as those inside stepped out onto the grass.

Her pulse quickened nervously. This was the moment they were to part ways.

She craned her head upwards, straining to see through a tiny crack in the wood. The sun was setting through the trees, but her friends were standing close enough that she caught little glimpses.

Seth was standing apprehensively before Cosette, watching as she knelt to the ground and slipped the salcor from her ankle. She held it a moment, fingers tightening nervously around the enchanted coil, then pressed it lightly into his hands.

"How's this for irony..." she teased, tensing in spite of herself as he knotted a loop and lifted it over her head. A second before it could fall she flinched away, cheeks burning in shame.

He paused immediately, staring down in concern.

"Sweetheart—"

"I'm sorry," she apologized quickly, squaring her shoulders and trying again. "It's just—"

"I know," he said quietly, lowering the slack to his side and gently cupping her cheek. Their eyes met in the dusky twilight. "I know *exactly* how this feels."

She stared a second longer, then shivered—allowing herself a single moment of fear.

"It's only me," he murmured, gazing steadily into her eyes. "I'm going to be standing by your side every moment. You'll only be wearing it a few hours, and the second you're released we'll use it to lasso that cousin of yours and drown him in the moat."

Cosette smiled in spite of herself, dropping her eyes to the ground. "All right."

A second later the rope circled around her neck.

No going back now...

Evie glanced at Ellanden, but his worried gaze was trained on Cosette.

"It should have been me," he muttered, shifting suddenly, as if preparing to break himself free. "This was a mistake. It could have been either of us, so why did we choose Cosette—"

"Because you *do* look like a threat," Evie soothed, taking his arm. "Jokes aside, Landi, we have a far better chance of this working if it's her and not you. She weighs about twenty pounds. She looks like a doll. And they're *still* binding her with the salcor, just because she's a fae."

Ellanden clenched his jaw, staring with grim determination at the floorboards. It was quiet for a few moments as the others continued their preparations, then he glanced over suddenly.

"Did he just call her sweetheart—"

"Let it go."

As the girls settled themselves strategically in the back of the wagon, Asher leapt lightly to the ground. According to the plan, he wouldn't be going with the others.

Which meant it was time to say goodbye.

"Hey, you."

Ellanden glanced down in surprise as the vampire's hand slipped through a tiny crack in the wood, sliding gently across his chest before coming to rest on his tunic. His thumb moved over the fabric, smoothing little circles as he leaned his forehead against the wagon with a sigh.

"I hate this," he murmured. "I hate not being able to see you. Not even to say goodbye."

APPROVAL

The princess bit her lip to keep from laughing, but the fae was simply bewildered. Asher may have come for a sweet farewell, but there was just one problem.

He had forgotten which person was on which side.

"Take care of yourself, all right?" His fingers tightened with a tender squeeze. "I worry about you so much, sometimes it feels like I can't breathe."

For a split second, the fae looked incredibly touched. The hand was disconcerting, and he'd just opened his mouth to reply, when the vampire said one last thing.

"I love you."

The words died on his tongue. Only then did he notice the princess was in convulsions.

A look of sudden understanding washed over him and he dropped his head to the floor, shaking with silent laughter. A second later, he reached up to touch the vampire's sleeve.

"I love you, too, Ash."

The hand disappeared.

The remaining time went by very fast. There were a few last-minute adjustments. Ellanden obsessively fidgeted with the nail. Freya vanished momentarily into the woods, then returned a moment later with a bright purple flower that she and Cosette smeared liberally on their mouths.

Having spent all his emotional currency on the fae, and feeling more than a little humiliated, Asher offered his girlfriend only a brisk, "Good luck," before heading into the trees alone.

She was still smiling about it when Seth hopped back onto the wagon.

"All right," he said quietly, "is everyone ready?"

That's when the smile disappeared.

We're really doing this. I can't believe we're really doing this.

They might technically have been away from home for the last ten years. But, like Freya said, it only felt like a few weeks. And despite their sudden rash of independence, a single word kept looping through her mind. *Unsupervised.* They'd had crazy ideas before, fantastically reckless plans that had come to define them. But they were never allowed to see them through.

In what dimension was this actually happening? One of them suggests that they storm the castle gates...then they *actually* storm the castle gates?

She could practically see her mother's disapproving scowl.

Not that she didn't storm a few castles of her own...

"We're ready," the girls chanted in unison.

"Ready," Evie echoed.

"Try to keep the cart on the road," Ellanden replied.

With no further notice than that the wagon began rumbling down the mountain path, carrying the group of unarmed teenagers towards the heavily armed fortress nestled near the top.

The princess drew in a silent breath, a little more frightened with every turn of the wheel.

Nope, there's no going back now...

Chapter 13

Things started off badly, not that anyone was really surprised. As fate would have it they weren't the only wagon on the road, and before they could make it to the gate of the fortress a cartload of goblins pulled up alongside. There was a brief argument, a flurry of words, but Seth didn't want to draw attention and conceded almost at once, backing up the horse to allow them through.

There were more problems at the gate.

"—telling you, I have an appointment!" an angry voice screeched somewhere up ahead of them. "So why don't you go find whoever's in charge—"

There was a sharp impact, followed by a vicious howl. A moment later the same wagon creaked dejectedly past them, heading back down the mountain.

Evie and Ellanden watched it roll past with wide eyes.

That bodes well.

"NEXT!"

Evie could almost feel Seth's hesitation as he eased the horse forward, coming to a stop at the gate. Soldiers appeared from both sides, looking the wagon carefully up and down.

"Good evening," he said politely. "I'm here to see Mallet."

A man who was apparently in charge took a step closer, gazing up at him with a scowl. "And do you have an appointment?"

The goblin's furious cry echoed in their ears.

In a decision that probably spared them all a great deal of pain Seth decided to come clean immediately, hopping off the wagon to put them at the same height.

"Not as such, and I know he's a busy man. I come on business from the Red Hand. I have two girls in the back he might be interested in. Jack sent me straight away."

Quick, concise, and he'd used all the right key words.

Red Hand. Jack. Girls.

The man's scowl disappeared immediately as he looked the young man up and down. He was clearly a shifter, one mannered enough not to have a death wish, and was styled in a similar way as many of Jack's wolves. Between that and the promise of new merchandise...

"Well that's another story, then," he said with a smile. "Let's take a look."

Together, the two of the circled around to the back of the cart—the soldiers following idly behind. Evie watched their silhouettes flicker past, hoping very much none of them had shifter blood themselves. The wagon creaked as Seth pulled back the canvas.

Sure enough, Cosette and Freya were propped up against the side of the cart—eyes closed, heads resting together, that strange purple stain fresh on their lips.

"Valerian," Seth volunteered, gesturing casually as if he did such things every day. "It was a long journey. I didn't want to be watching them every second."

The guard nodded as well—a man who *actually* did such things every day.

"That's a smart move," he murmured, peering at the closest girl. "What is she?" He flicked the bottom of Freya's shoe. "Shifter, witch—"

"Just a pretty girl," Seth said casually. It had been decided that a witch would raise red flags regardless of whether she was bound or not. "We always have need for those. I picked her up in one of the villages on my way over. Feisty, but harmless. I decided to bind the fae just in case."

Another key term. It did the trick.

"A fae?" the man repeated in surprise, stepping up onto the wheel. The wagon creaked to the side as he peered into the back for a better look. "Well, I'll be damned...Jack did this?"

"*I* did this," Seth corrected, with a note of pride. "It's why he's letting me make the transaction." There was a brief pause. "He also happens to be my uncle."

The man leaned back with a chuckle, nodding as if it all made sense. "I see...grooming you to take the reins one day?"

Seth flashed a tight smile. "So to speak."

"Well, I appreciate the consideration. Most of the kids we get from the village are skin and bones, barely able to manage a few days in the cells. But these girls are pretty, they'll go fast. And the fae..." His eyes sparked as his tongue ran slowly over his lips. "I might just keep her for myself."

Evie didn't have to see his face to imagine Seth's exact expression. She could only hope he had the wherewithal to curb it before the soldiers noticed it as well.

Apparently he did.

"For the right price," he answered evenly.

"Yes...for the right price. Let's get you inside." The man glanced over his shoulder, waving at the fort. "The sun's going down. You can stay the night here. Head back off in the morning."

Evie smirked to herself as they rolled forward. That was exactly the reason they'd left when they did. Early enough so as not to seem intentional. Late enough to merit an invitation to stay.

Without any further questions, they made their way into the fort.

The uneven dirt road gave way to something even worse—cobblestones. The refreshing smell of the forest gave way to charcoal dust and tar. Whatever the fort's original purpose, it hadn't yet buried those roots. There was a strange industrial feel to it—like stepping into a mine that was somehow above the surface. Nevertheless, the princess was feeling bizarrely upbeat.

For the first time since leaving, she had a flicker of hope. Maybe this wasn't such a crazy plan after all. They'd done the impossible. They'd made it inside. What could possibly go wrong?

"Hold up."

Seth paused as the man who'd originally detained them swept forward with a sword and a smile. An odd combination, and he used them both the same way.

"We got to talking back there and I almost forgot," he gestured to the wagon with the tip of his blade. "I need to check out the cart. Strictly business, you understand."

The shifter nodded quickly, looking pale. "Of course."

He hopped down again from the wooden seat and watched as the man moved in a slow circle around the wagon, pausing every so often to look it up and down. There wasn't much to check, the thing was rudimentary at best. But he moved slowly, reveling in the young man's nerves.

At long last he hopped into the cart itself, shifting the frame with every creaking step.

Evie could see him then—standing almost directly above her. A harsh-looking man in his mid-forties with a cropped grey beard and a smile that could easily turn cruel. He knelt down in front of the girls—both of whom were still pretending to be asleep. The smile flickered brighter when he lifted Cosette's chin with two fingers, examining the salcor tied around her neck.

He moved an inch or two closer. Ellanden looked like he was ready to explode.

Then Seth called from the back of the cart. "Is there a problem?"

The man straightened abruptly, getting to his feet. "No—no problem," he replied. "I'll have the men show you where to put them, and where you can sleep."

"We'll be staying together," Seth answered sharply. The man raised his eyebrows, but the shifter didn't back down. "Until they're sold, both of those girls are my responsibility. Look at their faces. You want me to leave them unsupervised in a garrison with your men?" He shook his head with a faint smile. "What would my uncle say?"

For a split second, Evie was scared they might come to blows. But after staring at him a moment, the man shook his head with a chuckle.

"Smart kid. I can see why he sent you."

"I do my best."

The man chuckled again and headed out to join him, pausing only a moment to complete the final step of his search. In a gesture that could only be described as routine, he gave his sword a cursory twirl then stabbed it down between the floorboards.

The first jab narrowly missed Ellanden's face. The second sank into Evie's shoulder.

Holy hell!

Pain blossomed across her body as a hand simultaneously clamped over her mouth. In the flickering light of the courtyard torches, she could just barely make out Ellanden's eyes—wide and terrified—begging her without words to keep quiet.

It was impossible. She bit down desperately on his hand.

Then as quickly as it had pierced her skin, the sword was leaving—sliding back up from the floorboards—covered in the princess' blood. In an act of desperation Ellanden's other hand flashed into the space between them, catching it lightly between two fingers, cleaning away the blood.

Silent tears spilled down her face. Her body was wracked with sobs.

I'm sorry! I'm sorry!

She could practically hear his silent cries.

Please, don't scream!

His fingers tightened over her mouth, but at the same time he brought their heads together—pressing a silent kiss to her temple, whispering straight into her ear.

"You're all right, you're all right," he chanted. "Just take a breath."

She tried but it was difficult, considering the weight of his hand. By the time she finally managed the man was gone, the girls had been unloaded, and they found themselves abruptly alone.

"...*ow*."

"Oh, honey," Ellanden kissed her again, smoothing damp hair off her forehead. "It really is going to be okay—I promise. The worst part's over, just try to breathe."

Each word was barely louder than a whisper, but she heard them all the same. Nevertheless, she'd been stabbed. She was bloody near inconsolable.

"It's-it's *not* okay," she whimpered, tears streaming down the side of her face. "It's a freakin' battle wound. And it's—" Her voice broke with a sob. "—it's all your fault!"

He made a quiet sound that could have been a laugh or a sigh.

"Okay, it can be my fault. Just don't bleed out on me, all right? Your boyfriend would be furious if you upset me. He sometimes can't breathe when I'm away."

Despite the pain, she found herself shaking with laughter—crying all the harder.

"You're such an arse-ling."

He ignored this, as he always did, and gave her hand a firm squeeze.

"And *you* are going to be fine—I promise." He leaned closer, taking a look for himself. "It might hurt, but it's not that deep. I wouldn't be surprised if you could still move that arm."

She wanted to snap at him, but he was right. There was some blood pooling on the wood between them, but the shock was already subsiding. She wiggled her fingers, one at a time.

That's just typical. We haven't left the wagon yet and I've already been stabbed.

"Now what?" she whispered, counting the seconds until the ordeal was over.

He closed his eyes with a sigh, doing the same thing. "Now...we wait."

THEY WERE BOTH SUPPOSED to stay sharp. It was an unspoken part of the plan. When you were locked in a smuggler's compartment behind enemy lines, you were supposed to stay sharp.

The princess promptly fell asleep.

I've been stabbed, she thought as she drifted off. She was entitled.

When she opened her eyes a few hours later everything was exactly as it had been before, only quieter. The wagon was still sitting in the corner of the courtyard, lit by only the occasional flicker of torches and the light of the moon. Whatever soldiers who weren't on duty had stopped socializing and gone to bed. Ellanden was lying beside her, staring unblinkingly at the sky.

And her shoulder still hurt. A *lot*.

"This is intolerable," she hissed, shifting fitfully and pressing her fingers to the wound. "As soon as we fulfill this bloody prophecy, I'm banning all swords from the High Kingdom. Belarians won't listen, pack of stubborn mutts, but I can probably get my mother on board. We're all going to become pacifists. We're going to treat our bodies like the temples that they are."

The fae glanced over with a faint smile. "Hello to you, too."

"I'm serious, Ellanden. Don't argue with me." She sniffed self-righteously, wallowing in all the blood. "As soon as we ban the swords we're going to roam the countryside, decapitating slavers, dismantling wagons, and burning every fortress to the ground."

"You might *need* some swords for that..."

"I'm serious," she insisted. "This was one of those things, Landi. One of those serious things that makes you take a step back and pause. You know what I'm going to do?"

"You're going to turn your life around?"

"I'm going to turn my life around!"

"Shocker."

"Life is about connections," she mused. "Connecting with other people, forcing them to connect with you. When things get back to normal, I'm going to host regular sit-ins at the castle for people to discuss their feelings. I'm going to learn several instruments and try to cook. I'm also going to have the physician teach me some basic first aid."

He opened his mouth to reply, then glanced at her in surprise.

"Considering what I know about you, that last part was actually rather sane."

"I'm *serious*, Ellanden."

"So you've said." He paused, and then added, "A few times."

The conversation fell apart as they both turned away, smiling. Encased in their dark little tomb, it was easy to pretend that none of this was happening. That they were lying on a bed, or in the grass, or on a castle roof, staring up at the stars like they'd done so many times before.

"Do you think that could actually happen?" he asked suddenly. "I mean, even if we all make it through this and reunite with our family...do you think anything will ever be the same?"

It was hard to consider such a thing impartially, especially when she and the others still found themselves living ten years in the past. She'd like very much to think that it would. This new world was jarring and terrible, and all the things she used to love most seemed to have faded away.

And yet part of her was afraid it wasn't so simple. Bend things long enough and they didn't just break, they formed new pieces. She wasn't sure those pieces could ever fit quite the same.

"Yeah, Ellanden. Absolutely."

Their eyes met in the darkness, then he turned away with a smile.

APPROVAL

It was impossible to lie to a fae. Even though he was only half, the same rules seemed to apply. It was a game they'd played together many times before.

"You should stop fiddling with that," he murmured, staring up at the wooden slats as she fretted at her shoulder, staining her hand with fresh blood. "You'll only make it worse."

She shook her head fervently. "I'm fixing it. I have great instincts for these sorts of things."

He sighed, feeling that claustrophobia all over again. "You have terrible instincts for these sorts of things. Why do you think I've never—"

She suddenly clapped a hand over his mouth, splattering his face with blood.

"Quiet!"

Someone was approaching the carriage. Someone who wasn't carrying a torch, moving as if they didn't want to be seen. At least, she could have sworn there was someone. When she listened for them a second later, there was nothing. It was as if they'd just disappeared.

Ellanden pried her fingers loose with a dark glare, then the two of them stared fearfully up at the floorboards. His fingers twitched reflexively towards the nail he'd been loosening—their back-up plan if anything should go wrong. Should he open it now? Should they take their chances—

At once, the plank vanished and they huddled together with a silent scream. Asher was standing triumphantly above them, the radiant smile already fading from his face.

"What the—?! What happened?" he whispered, staring down in horror.

It must have been a rather ghastly sight.

The princess had been stabbed in the shoulder. The fae had a bloody handprint clapped across his face. They stared back in stunned silence, then reached out their hands at the same time.

"Yeah, yeah—I've got you."

The vampire pulled them swiftly from the hidden compartment, gawking another moment at the stains of blood. His hands travelled automatically to his girlfriend, but there wasn't time. The moon was already directly above them. The others would be waiting inside.

"The guards are gone?" Ellanden asked, eyes flickering through the slit in the canvas to the stone walkway circling high above. The silhouette of a soldier stared back at him, and he jerked back with a start. "Ash, didn't you—"

"I did," Asher interrupted swiftly. "All of them."

It was an impossible feat. It was impossible not to have a bit of pride. Yet the vampire was strangely pragmatic, talking in casual tones about things that made the others pause.

"I left some of the bodies behind," he explained. "Propped them up to look more realistic."

His friends went blank.

...gross.

"That's great, babe," Evie said with forced cheer. "Really...creative."

Ellanden cast her a look. "Maybe he can come to one of your sit-ins. Work on all those twisted feelings."

Asher glanced confusedly between them. "What?"

"No time."

Without another word Evie took both men by the wrist and pulled them carefully out of the wagon, crouching down immediately to hide in its shadow. Seth had done well to steer it into the corner. From this vantage point, they could take in the entire courtyard without being seen.

"They offered Seth a room, but he refused it—said he would stay with the girls," Evie caught Asher up under her breath. "Instead of thinking they'd just let Cosette and Freya stay with him up there, I'm guessing they're forcing all of them to sleep down in the dungeon."

Ellanden made a dangerous sound under his breath, while Asher nodded swiftly.

APPROVAL

"Then the dungeon is where we need to go."

Without a whisper of sound they streaked across the shadowy stone to the nearest doorway, taking down any guards who happened to venture into their path. Evie knocked a man unconscious and locked him in a closet. Asher slipped behind another and snapped his neck, while Ellanden clapped his hand over the mouth of a third and smashed his head straight through stone fountain.

The other two stared at the wreckage.

"Someone's still touchy he was smuggled in the wagon," Asher remarked casually.

The fae flashed him a quick grin. "Next time, I'd prefer to ride on top."

The three friends raced down the never-ending stairwell, hearts pounding with adrenaline, terrified at any moment to hear the clang of the bell. The air grew damp the lower they went, a strange sulfuric smell wafting up from somewhere beneath the floor.

"What was this place?" Evie panted, gripping her shoulder as she struggled to keep up.

Asher threw a glance behind him then swept her lightly into his arms, continuing down the stairs without ever breaking pace. "I thought it was a garrison. The location, the design...all of that would make sense. But the inside is different. The inside is strange."

Unwilling to dwell too deeply on those comments, they continued their downward spiral until the ground leveled suddenly and they came to a stop.

There were voices in the corridor. And laughter. Lots of laughter.

The plan had been relatively simple. Seth would use his connection to the Red Hand to take the girls inside as prisoners, smuggling Evie and Ellanden through the gate as well. Asher would spirit himself over the wall and take out the upper level of soldiers before the three of them joined the rest in the dungeon to free the prisoners and stage their great escape.

They had assumed the guards would be minimal. They had assumed Seth and the others would be pretending to be asleep. They had been wrong.

What they found instead was a party.

The cells were stuffed with drowsy prisoners awaiting auction, but no fewer than fifty well-trained soldiers had crammed themselves in the hallway in between. A table had been dragged down from the kitchens and nine men were seated in a circle as the rest of them drank and cheered.

One of those men was Seth.

He was still in his travelling clothes and was staring with fierce concentration at something in his hands. Unlike the others, his drink was almost completely full. He was also having a difficult time tuning out their bedraggled audience, though at every moment he kept a careful smile on his face.

He glanced up as the others appeared in the doorway. The soldiers glanced up as well.

For a single moment, everything was silent.

Then he lifted his shoulder in a helpless shrug.

"They wanted to play cards."

Seven hells.

There was no delay between those five words and what happened next. Nor did the soldiers waste any time in deducing that Seth was apparently acquainted with the people at the door. Unlike some of the mindless brutes the friends had fought before these men had discipline, they had training, and they knew without a shadow of a doubt that they hadn't been cleared to come inside.

That made them a danger. It made them a threat.

And every soldier in that fortress knew how to handle a threat.

With a wild cry they launched themselves forward, drawing their weapons as the friends stepped back in surprise. None of them had been prepared for the onslaught—they were still blinking in disorientation, trying to reconcile the large group of people gathered beneath the dim lights.

Unfortunately, there wasn't time for any of that.

Evie was struck in the face before she saw the man standing in front of her. He hadn't used his hands but the grip of his sword. While the men were most likely to be dispatched and dumped into the moat as a warning, she was young woman and far more likely to fetch a price.

The thought of it made her blood boil.

Before he could lift the sword to strike her again she spun low right where she was standing, catching him off balance and yanking the blade right out of his hand. He was stumbling backwards when she whirled around to face him, stabbing a deep hole in the center of his chest.

It was easy. Almost fun. They were slavers, after all.

Then she clutched her shoulder with a pitiful cry.

"Evie!"

Asher's head spun around the second he heard the noise, searching for her desperately in the riotous crowd. Most people would hesitate to confront a vampire. Most people had involuntary heart palpitations the second they saw the fangs. But said vampire was in cramped quarters, vastly outnumbered, and the guards had been drinking enough to make them cocky.

Needless to say, Asher was having troubles of his own.

The second he was distracted, one of the soldiers ripped a torch from a rusted sconce and shoved the flames right into his face. At the same time two more kicked the table in his direction, pinning him roughly against the wall. He gasped softly at the impact. There were massive holes in his vision from the blinding flames. One hand lifted instinctively as the other braced against the table, but before he could make any progress five more guards leapt right on top of it—holding onto the wall for balance while kicking the vampire right in the face.

Evie froze in horror.

She sometimes forgot that vampires weren't invincible. She sometimes forgot that these things were all a question of age. Her uncles regularly fought each other with cheerful abandon, and Cassiel had won as many matches against Aidan as he lost. If you were to ask him, quite a few more.

Asher let out a cry, throwing both arms in front of his face. His feet slipped against the floor, but the heavy table kept him standing. And those boots kept on hammering him, landing viciously again and again, giving no time to recover and ripping open any unguarded skin.

"Ash!"

The princess threw herself towards him, only to have three giant men beat her back. She lifted her sword on instinct, fending them off, but the most she could do was stand her ground. A part of her wanted desperately to shift, but they were in an enclosed space—with a dozen cages that needed to be opened—and she had no idea when she might suddenly need her hands.

Fortunately, she wasn't the only one who'd heard the vampire's cry.

Ellanden didn't just glance up when he heard his friend was in trouble, he moved himself at the same time—flipping in a graceful arc until he was standing beside the soldiers on the table. They didn't notice him at first—they were so preoccupied with kicking Asher's face in. But he announced himself as only a true Prince of the Fae ever could.

There were five screams. Five horrifyingly intimate sword thrusts that burned themselves forever into the princess' mind. Then five bodies fell to the floor.

"...Landi?"

The fae leapt off the table at once, yanking it away from the vampire before flying back in time to catch him as he stumbled forward. The room swam dizzily as Asher gripped his shoulders hard, blinking in a daze. The battle was still raging, but he couldn't see past the bodies.

...what was *left* of the bodies.

"What did you do to them?" he asked slowly, unable to look away.

Ellanden threw a careless glance over his shoulder. "I rearranged them a little," he said dismissively. "Like they were doing to your face."

When dealing with the Fae, it was best to judge them solely on their intentions. Asher held back the first two things that came to mind and settled for a simple, "That's sweet. Thanks."

The prince flashed a bright smile, and together they threw themselves back into the fray.

The fight was getting dirtier the longer it carried on. There had been heavy casualties on both sides, but fatalities on only one. As the odds slowly evened themselves out, those soldiers who remained were spurring themselves on even harder. Taking greater risks and surprising their young opponents with sudden bursts of recklessness, tempered with finely polished steel.

They were focused on one man in particular.

"Clever kid, sneaking past the gate."

Two soldiers grabbed Seth by the arms as another punched him full in the face. He let out a broken gasp and slumped in their arms, spitting out a mouthful of blood.

"But you don't stand a chance of getting back out of here." The man punched him again with such force, Evie suspected he'd lost some money at cards. "You'll just end up in a cage."

Seth nodded distractedly, flexing his hands into fists. "A cage, huh?"

His eyes lifted slowly, settling on the man's face.

"You know, some of my friends are in that cage," he said softly. "Not too long ago, I was in a cage myself. And while I hate to spoil the fun you're having, I have no intention of going back."

What happened next was hard to describe.

Every fight had rules. The people fighting him played by those rules. But it was like no one had ever explained them to Seth. Because from the moment he tore free of the people holding him, there was truly nothing in the world that could stand in his way.

The others froze in their tracks, staring in quiet amazement.

It was hard to see him, exactly. It was easier to follow his movements by the trail of carnage he left in his wake. The sounds ringing in the cavern escalated wildly then began to temper into a quiet din, one that lessened by the moment as more and more soldiers fell to the floor.

Still, he kept going. Tearing through them without mercy. Finishing each with such brutal, exacting vengeance that Evie had a sudden, bizarre flashback of the day they'd found him again Tarnaq—decapitating demons to the delight of a bloodthirsty crowd. Like something out of a dream, the voice of the announcer was ringing in her ears.

Ladies and gentlemen...I give you our champion!

"I don't know, Landi." Asher nudged him with a little smile. "You sure you want to get on his bad side? Might be time to extend an olive branch."

The fae shot him a look, but said nothing.

After only a few minutes, there was only a single guard left. Fifty whittled down to one. The friends advanced on him slowly, watching as he backed in terror towards the cells.

"You have something we're looking for," Seth told him, with a disturbingly friendly smile.

"The keys," Asher said curtly. "Hand them over."

To be fair, there was a chance the man might actually have done so if he weren't so terrified. A spasm of fear rippled over him and he backed away, silent as a grave.

Ellanden sighed impatiently, throwing a glance at the ceiling.

"Look—I can literally *see* them right there." He gestured to a brass ring clasped to the man's belt. "Any second, your friends are going to ring that damn bell. So if you could just expedite—"

The man drew his sword.

You're an idiot.

"You won't get away with this!" he bellowed like a wounded dog.

Ellanden rolled his eyes. "Oh, we're *absolutely* going to get away with it."

The man lunged forward, but Seth kicked him back with a snarl. He clattered against the bars of the cage, still spluttering his threats, when a pair of slender arms wrapped around his neck.

Cosette materialized out of the darkness like a vengeful ghost, staring at the back of the man's head like she wanted to bite him. Her arms tightened and his face went from red to blue.

He let out a shriek as she whispered in his ear, lips stained with a false tint of Valerian.

"This is for Lottie, and Emile, and Savannah, and a lot of other friends I made during my time here." With her free hand, she took the keys from his waistband and tossed them to Seth. "You don't need these. Where you're going, no one bothers to lock the doors..."

A final jerking motion, and the man fell dead at her feet.

Somewhere high above them, a bell clanged in the night. It was followed by a chorus of distant shouts and boots on cobblestone. Any moment the soldiers were going to realize the trouble was in the dungeons, not at the gate. They could not still be there when that happened.

The doors to the cells burst open as Seth worked the keys. A dozen or so people ventured forth. Most looked like they knew him. Most looked like they couldn't believe their eyes.

"Seth?" A young man hobbled towards the front of the group, shivering cold and weak from hunger. "What are you—"

"There isn't time." The shifter clapped him gently on the shoulder, making a quick assessment of the rest of them. "Think you can do me a favor? In just a second, do you think you can use that table to barricade the door?"

The boy's eyes drifted across the bloody dungeon.

"Yeah. I can do that."

The shifter squeezed him again then he and the rest of the friends headed quickly back to the stairwell, drawing their blades as they went. The boy's eyes widened and he called out again.

"What are you guys going to do?"

Seth threw a quick smile over his shoulder. "We're going to take back this fort."

Chapter 14

In the dungeon, there were about fifty soldiers. In the courtyard, there were about two hundred. By all accounts, the dungeon should have been the easier fight. The courtyard should have been next to impossible. But the friends had something they didn't have in the dungeon.

They had magic.

"You know how I'm always telling you to be careful when you practice?" Asher asked softly, watching as an endless swarm of soldiers thundered their way. "To hold back a little?"

Evie nodded quickly, trying to catch her breath. "Yeah?"

Their eyes met and he flashed a little smile.

"Go crazy."

A sudden burst of heat blossomed over the princess' hands, and with those two words ringing in her ears she let loose a wave of fire that would have made her mother proud.

It arced in giant waves over the cobblestones, bouncing with a strange lightness before descending on the swarm like it had a mind of its own. There wasn't really time to scream, though some of the soldiers managed to do it anyway. It was a testament to how fast it happened, that in a blind panic some of them continued racing forward. Most of these were on fire. Those who weren't were cut down by her friends before they made it halfway across the stones.

After only a few seconds, the crimson flames were joined by another color. Freya dropped her sword and raised both hands, standing shoulder to shoulder with the princess as they rained down hell on the fort. It was easier than they could have imagined. And utterly exhausting as well.

"Seven hells," Evie gasped as the last man fell in a crumbling heap of ash. In a beat of knee-jerk irony, she fell to the ground as well. "I could sleep a thousand years."

"Don't make jokes about that," Ellanden cautioned as Asher knelt beside her.

"You were incredible," he murmured, pressing a soft kiss to her forehead. "Seriously, love, I don't know how you do it."

Freya plopped down beside them, shaking the smoke from her hands.

"She learned a lot of it from me," she said casually, flicking a stray flame off the tip of her shoe. "We're developing one of those poetic master-apprentice relationships."

Evie chuckled with exhaustion, then stopped quickly when she saw Asher's face.

"What happened to you?" she blurted before she could stop herself.

There wasn't a mark on him. The man had been nearly kicked to death by half a dozen soldiers and there wasn't a single mark on his body. He looked just as he always did. Steady, composed, and entirely too beautiful for a teenage girl to know what to do with.

...with a generous helping of dried blood.

"Did you—"

She cut herself off before she could finish. Not that she needed to. The second she opened her mouth to ask the question, Asher's cheeks flushed with a hint of shame.

He fed from one of the soldiers. It's probably how he killed the man.

In spite of how many times they'd fought together in the past, she'd never really considered him doing something like this. Using his fangs as weapons. Just like a real vampire fought.

A real vampire.

She chided herself just for thinking it. She was no better than the rest of them, pinning her boyfriend into an impossible corner. Too rough for one side, too polished for the other. Eternally penalized for the mere inconvenience of having discovered his soul.

She was glad his face was no longer broken. She would leave it at that.

"Well, I guess we can go get the rest of them," Ellanden stifled a yawn, shaking out the arm that had been holding his sword. "Tell them it's safe to come out."

"I still can't believe we did it," Seth murmured, looking out at the fort. "Slavers have been stealing people from my village since I was a child...no one's ever come back."

Cosette peeled herself off the wall, resting a hand on his shoulder.

For a few minutes, the friends followed his gaze—staring at the bloody courtyard. Now that the fighting was done, it was strangely peaceful. The moon lit the stone with a silver glow. A gentle breeze rippled through the surrounding trees.

"Why do they need to come back?" Evie asked suddenly, pushing herself off the ground. A group of blank faces stared back at her. "I'm serious—why go back to the village when there's a perfectly good, well-fortified, conveniently empty place to live right here?"

For a second, the only thing that registered was shock. Then one by one the friends started to smile. Seth was the last to break, staring at the fortress with an expression she'd never quite seen.

They shared a fleeting look, then she cocked her head towards the gate with a smile.

"Saves you the trouble of fixing that roof..."

※

THE VERY NEXT NIGHT, Seth's pack had a proper feast. A feast with tables and chairs on cobblestone. A feast lit by a ring of torches and protected by a heavily reinforced gate. A feast boasting everything a pack of highly-skilled wolves was able to hunt between the fort and the old village.

And it was indeed the old village.

Because those villagers were officially living somewhere new.

It was good that it had taken so long for them to pack and make the journey, because when Seth and Cosette set out the next morning to get them the fortress still looked like a tomb. Almost three hundred bodies littered the ground in various states and pieces, and the smooth grey stone was covered in enough blood to make parts look as though it had simply been painted red.

As the villagers packed, the friends spent the day ferrying corpses to the woods and scrubbing enemy blood from the walls. In a fit of rebellion, Freya had suggested they simply dump everyone over the side into the moat. That's what moats were for, she claimed. But after a brief lesson about hospitality and reminding her that the bodies would float, they continued their grisly task. The only silver lining was that they weren't working alone.

At first, they'd been appalled by the prisoners' offers to help. Don't trouble yourselves, they'd said. Get some rest, they'd said. But each and every person who'd been locked in those cells took a grim kind of delight in gathering up the pieces of their captors and burying them in a shallow grave.

They were just finishing the gruesome task, when one of the younger boys from the village ran across the courtyard, screaming at the top of his lungs, "They're here! They're here!"

The gate opened. The drawbridge came down. And the villagers emerged from the forest.

As long as Evie lived, she'd never forget the looks on their faces.

"Pass the ale."

The princess jerked back to the present to see Freya holding out her goblet, waving it in the air with a tipsy grin. The soldiers hadn't just liked to play cards. They'd liked to drink as well. In the process of clearing the lower levers, the friends had stumbled across a cache of alcohol that had made Seth close his eyes with a smile and Ellanden thank the fates for finally giving them a bit of luck.

"Are you sure?" Evie asked, handing over the pitcher. "You look a little dizzy already."

"How dare you," the witch replied in a deadpan. "After I single-handedly liberated a fort."

Asher chuckled, pouring another helping into her glass. "She's right, the girl deserves a drink." He gave his girlfriend a wink. "So do you."

Meanwhile, an impromptu confession was happening at the far end of the table.

"Darren told me what happened," Charlotte was saying quietly, holding tight to her son's hand. "What your uncle did…some of the things you did yourself."

Evie's head jerked up with a start. Suddenly she realized why Seth had been so hesitant to tell his mother the full story. In revealing his uncle's guilt, he'd have to confess his own as well.

"I…" He trailed off, pale as a sheet. "I didn't…"

She squeezed his hand with a motherly smile. "Sweetheart, we may live in the middle of nowhere but do you really think I've never heard of the Red Hand? You were doing what you had to." She shushed him when he tried to protest, cupping his cheek. "You were doing all you could to provide for me and your sisters."

He bowed his head with a shuddering sigh. She touched her forehead to his.

There were several other highlights of the evening.

The first came when Freya accidentally ingested some of the Valerian smeared around her mouth and ended up face-planting in the middle of dinner. Another came when several members of the village stepped forward to present Ellanden with a gift.

He lifted his head in surprise, setting down his glass.

"What's this?"

Charlotte stood up from the table with a smile.

"This is for you," she answered, placing it in his hands, "with my eternal thanks. Seth told me what you did in the grasslands. How you threw him to safety, taking the fall yourself." Her voice hitched and her eyes shone with tears. "You saved my son's life, Ellanden. I will never forget it."

Evie leaned forward, trying to see for herself. It was a bow, she realized. Crudely made, hacked from the nearest tree, but put together by the most loving hands. The others braced as he took it, knowing his imperious standards. But his face warmed with a true smile.

"I'm honored."

The crowd dispersed, returning to their meal. But he was still looking at it, running his fingers up and down the knotted crescent with a lingering smile.

That smile faded slightly when he saw Seth watching.

"Let's be clear, dog. I didn't mean to save your life," he snapped, setting the bow carefully on the table in front of him. "If we're being honest, I would rather it hadn't happened."

"I know that," Seth replied, gesturing to the bow. "I told them not to give it to you."

Both men stared at each other a moment before turning away, hiding secret smiles.

But Evie would always remember that night for a different reason.

"Take a walk with me..."

She hadn't realized Asher was standing behind her until his cool breath tickled her ear. Her breathing hitched and she pushed back her chair, heading after him. She expected him to head into the forest, but he didn't. He started climbing instead. She followed him up the winding stairwells until they reached the very top of the fort—the little bell tower that had caused them so much grief.

"Seven hells...it's beautiful."

She folded her arms on the railing, leaning over.

Everyone looked so small from such a distance. Just tiny playthings hosting a festive dinner in a toy fort. She could barely hear their quiet laughter as it drifted up on the breeze.

"They deserve this," she murmured, gazing down with a smile. "More than anyone I think I've ever met. They deserve to have a home."

Asher flashed her a quick look, then nodded in silence.

"What?" she asked.

He glanced at her again, surprised she'd noticed.

"Nothing—you're right." He stared down at the villagers, dancing in the light of the fire. "They deserve a home. Everyone deserves a home."

The quiet words clenched a knot in her chest and her eyes flickered sideways, resting a moment on his face. He was smiling, yes, but he was also incurably sad. In a moment of horrible recognition, she realized it was an expression he wore quite often.

"Asher—"

"Do you have any idea what it's been like?" he interrupted quietly. "Travelling around all these years with my father? Spending my life growing up at other people's palaces?"

She caught her breath. "I never knew you wanted a palace."

"Not a palace—a *home*." He turned to face her, putting his back to the village. "My entire life, Evie, I've never had one. And yes, staying with you and Ellanden was warm and familiar. And yes, the two of you are more my family than if we were actual blood—but all that was yours."

He shook his head with that sad smile.

"It was never mine."

She wanted to deny it. She wanted to scream that it wasn't true.

But it was.

The looks he got wherever they went, the empty plate night after night at the dinner table. Slowing down his movements for the sake of his friends. Mothers covering their children's eyes.

Suddenly, she couldn't blame him for wanting to explore the vampires' secret cavern within the mountain. She couldn't begrudge him the flash of excitement when they'd jumped off the ledge.

It couldn't be priced, that sense of belonging.

"Diana and her people have done terrible things," he said quietly, dark eyes flashing up to hers. "You think I don't know they've done terrible things? But as much as it haunts me, vampires have been doing terrible things since the dawn of time." His eyes dilated and his voice trembled with intensity. "But for the first time, maybe for the first time *ever*, they're doing something else as well."

He shook his head slowly, piecing the words together.

"It might not be perfect. Parts of it might still be seeped in innocent blood, but Evie...it *is* a change. They're changing. And maybe one day..." He caught himself, staring longingly down at the village. "Maybe one day we could have something like this, too."

A sudden silence fell between them. For a long while, he didn't seem to notice. Then he took her hand shyly, afraid he might have said too much.

"Does that make any sense?"

She stared back at him a moment.

"Yes, it does."

He let out a breath, unaware he'd been holding it. But before he could look up again, she stretched up on her toes and kissed him. He froze instinctively, then pulled back in surprise.

"What was..." He stared down at her, trying to interpret the sudden change. "I'm sorry, I didn't mean to bring you up here and then complain—"

She kissed him again.

"I just wanted to get away from the noise for a while. See the view—"

Another kiss.

"Not that I wasn't having fun at the—"

APPROVAL

This time he caught her, holding her there. Their fingers tangled in each other's hair as they stumbled backwards against the stone railing. He set her on top of it without thinking, bringing them to eye level, and her legs curved around his waist. Two hands wrapped behind his neck and she pulled him as close as she possibly could...then bit down suddenly on his lip.

He burst out laughing, stepping back in surprise.

"Don't start that game, princess. You won't win."

She slid off the railing, suddenly serious. "I don't want to win," she said softly. "I want to be with you."

The smile froze on his face as he stared down at her, trying to understand. At first, he thought it was simply physical. He moved where she directed, stepping closer when she tugged on his sleeve. Then she lifted a finger and touched the tiny dot of blood on his lips.

"I want to be with you," she said again.

Absolute. Shock.

His mouth fell open and he took a quick step back. In the courtyard beneath them, the party was still going. But the world in the little bell tower was quiet and still.

"You can't...you can't mean that."

She stared calmly into his eyes. "I've thought about it for a long time. It's something I want to do."

Silence.

He couldn't seem to find any words. He couldn't even seem to breathe. Looking back on it later, she probably shouldn't have proposed such a thing so dangerously high off the ground. In his present state, there was honestly no telling what might happen.

After a few agonizing seconds, he bowed his head.

"I've...I've never shared blood with anyone."

She couldn't help but smile. Never had she seen him so undone. "Asher Dorsett, I'm your best friend. Do you think I don't know that?"

He relaxed ever so slightly, then tensed again when he looked at her. "We've always talked about...I mean...we had never planned to bond." His eyes searched hers in the moonlight, trying to read her thoughts. "I didn't think you wanted something like that."

"Do *you* want something like that?"

There was a long pause.

"Yes," he admitted softly. "But that shouldn't have any bearing on—"

She lifted her finger to her mouth. He caught her swiftly by the wrist.

"Evie—"

"I want this."

"...it's forever."

"I want this forever. I want *you* forever." She placed both hands on the sides of his face, staring up into his eyes. "Asher...I can be your home."

They kissed in the moonlight, the blood still on his lips.

Her mouth flew open with a gasp as there was a sudden rush of sensation. Her eyes flew open in wonder, and it felt like she was rising straight off the ground.

As it turned out, she was...right into his arms.

"I think I fell in love with you when I was dreaming," he whispered, brushing back her long hair. "I think for ten years, I slept with you cradled in my arms."

A tear slipped down her face. He kissed it away.

Then they lay down beneath the giant bell and started taking off their clothes...

EVIE GOT UP EARLY THE next morning, just as the sun was rising over the trees. She took one look at Asher, still sleeping beside her, and decided not to wake him. He looked too perfect, eyes closed and lips gently parted, black hair fanning around him like a crooked halo.

Besides, he hadn't gotten much sleep.

With a smile she couldn't control, she dressed quickly and slipped outside—heading down the stone steps to the courtyard below. Maybe it was residual energy from the bond, maybe she was just *unbelievably* happy, but she'd decided to head into the forest for a while to hunt. After all, the pack had severely dented their supply at the feast. They'd be needing to replenish it—

"Morning!"

She jumped around with a gasp, to see Ellanden smiling just a few feet back. He caught up with her quickly, pushing open the gate to let them both through.

"And where are you off to?" she asked brightly.

He glanced down with a grin. "Thought I might test out my new bow. What about you? Off to hunt?"

Am I that obvious?

"But with no weapons," he said suddenly, coming to a stop. They were just on the other side of the drawbridge, a stone's throw from the trees. "Did you...were you planning to shift?" He paused, then gestured back to the courtyard. "I could do my thing later—"

"No, not at all!" she said quickly. In truth she *had* been planning to shift, but she'd much rather have the company. "Do you have a knife or something I could use?"

"Yeah—here."

For the next few minutes the two of them walked in silence, strolling beneath the sunlit trees, leaving all their cares deliberately behind them. It wasn't hard to do. For the first time they had shelter, food, and access to weapons. Lots of weapons. No more magical portals or enchanted rivers that led them to rodent-infested bogs. They had a grip on something. They could make a plan.

Later.

For now, the princess had several other things on her mind...

Was this normal? Had they stepped into a particularly vibrant set of trees? The colors were shocking in their beauty. Striking sapphires, emeralds so deep and rich they melted into shimmering pools of green. Wild mint and rosemary grew side by side, tickling her nose as she trailed her fingers through a whisper of lilacs. And then there was the sex.

Yes, she'd done that. And she couldn't go more than a few steps without replaying the words 'and then there was the sex' as her mind circled back to it.

Maybe it was the blood. The blood was making the colors brighter, the blood was responsible for that impossible night she'd shared with Asher just a few hours before.

He swore it was always like that. Then he offered to show her.

Again and again and again.

A mischievous smile crept up her face as she tilted back her head and stared at everything around her. It took a little while to realize that Ellanden was staring at her instead.

"What's going on with you?" he asked, smiling as well. "You're different this morning."

She looked away with a start, shaking her head quickly. "What—nothing. I'm just...happy about how things turned out, that's all."

His eyes followed every step.

"With the fort, I mean. I'm happy about how things turned out with the fort." She drummed her fingers against her legs, babbling uncontrollably. "We couldn't have given it to nicer people, and it's really great that none of us happened to die. All in all, there's just a lot to be grateful for—"

He pulled her to a sudden stop.

For a second, it was quiet. He simply looked her up and down with those inquisitive dark eyes. Then his lips parted with sudden understanding, and he was the one to look away.

"Wow..." he murmured, moving once more through the trees. "All that death and bloodshed was really a turn-on, huh?" Her cheeks flamed with a blush, but he was smiling. "Unless—"

He stopped again suddenly, a far different expression on his face.

"Unless...you did a little more than that?"

She didn't answer. She couldn't answer. When she did nothing but stand there, he reached out hesitantly and gave the top of her arm a gentle squeeze.

"Your shoulder is healed."

An answer all to itself.

They both stood there, suddenly unsure what to say.

"You wanted to?" he asked tentatively. "You both wanted to?"

It was a fair question. Blood bonds were never to be taken lightly. Even the most practiced of participants were known to get swept away.

She nodded slowly, looking into his eyes.

"Yeah, we both wanted to."

They stared a moment longer, then his lips quirked with a little smile.

"It was a good night, then."

Her face broke into another beaming grin.

"Yeah, it was a really good night."

They walked a while longer, lost to their thoughts as they made their way through the trees. Every so often he'd glance down at the top of her head with a secret smile. Every so often she'd bite down on her lip, re-contemplating the words, 'and then there was the sex'.

After a long time, she broke the silence with a sudden question.

"Do you think Asher wants to have children?"

The fae almost tripped in alarm. "Seven hells, please do *not* get ahead of yourself—"

"Give me a break," she swatted him. "I'm just asking."

With the exception of Cosette, Asher had been largely indifferent to children. He liked them, but from a distance. Like he'd always considered them as something separate from himself.

But he'd been different back at the village, seeing possibilities where he hadn't before.

"I think Asher might consider having children...several decades from now." Ellanden shot her a sharp look. "When we're bored enough to convince ourselves that it might be a good idea."

"This isn't about having children," she mused, distractedly moving a few steps ahead. "It's just...things are changing, you know? *He's* changing. The two of us...we're changing together."

We're changing together?

She came to a sudden stop.

"...did I honestly just say that?"

Ellanden chuckled, draping an arm around her shoulders. "Relax. It was your first time."

She wanted to fire back, but there was that smile again. Ruining all her pithy comebacks, making her stupid and happy until it decided to go away.

And in the meantime...

"A vampire kid would be strange," she thought out loud, stomping loudly through the dense underbrush. "That one back in the mountain tried to bite my hand."

Ellanden laughed again, releasing her to fiddle with his bow. "That's just kids, Everly. When we were kids, *I* tried to bite your hand."

She grinned in spite of herself, running her fingers along the trees. "Yeah, but you've always had really poor self-control—"

It hit her like a battering ram, sending her straight off the little ledge they'd been walking on and down into the ravine. Stars exploded behind her eyes as a sharp sting laced up the side of her neck. She could hear Ellanden shouting. One hand flew out to find him.

But the fae was about to have problems of his own.

The second he took a step towards her, there was a wrenching metallic sound as a device that resembled a giant bear trap clamped suddenly around his waist. He let out a horrible cry as one of the blades stabbed into him, burying itself in his chest not far from where the Carpathian dagger had torn him open not long before. A single ringing cry, then he slumped over it—broken and trembling, unable to move for the astonishing pain ripping open his chest.

"Evie," he whispered, unable to make it louder than that. "Help…"

HE DIDN'T REMEMBER prying the teeth away from him. He didn't remember how he got to the tree. It was morning when he lost consciousness, and when he opened his eyes again it was mid-day.

And he wasn't alone.

"What's this?"

He lifted his head weakly, squinting into the sun. Two blurry figures stepped out of the forest and came to a stop in front of him. Hands on their hips. Making no effort to help.

"See—I told you!" One of them slapped the other in delight. "We always find something good when we take the eastern trail. And you wanted to head south."

Ellanden stared in a daze between them, one hand braced tightly against his chest.

The shorter of the men was coming towards him now, kneeling down with an appraising expression. But he leapt back almost immediately, scrambling back in alarm.

"He's Fae," he said warily, taking another step back.

"He's young," the other answered, staring evenly at the prince. "Almost a child."

"He could have been a child for a long time, is my point—"

"Let's take a look."

There was a silent power struggle as the two men shared a look. After a few seconds, the more reluctant let out a sigh and knelt down once more. His eyes swept the fae up and down, wide with wonder, before he reached out curiously and tried to move his arm.

Ellanden let out a quiet moan, blood soaking through his tunic.

"Seven hells—he's going to bleed out before we get him to the market!"

"No, he won't." The other man knelt down quickly beside them. "Fae are strong. Quick healers. We brace him up with something and he'll be fine—at least until the buyer takes him away."

...*the buyer?*

Ellanden murmured something in his native tongue, trying to hold on to the tree when they reached for him. Just a second later he slumped over in defeat, head bowed to his chest.

"Bind his hands."

With an almost apologetic grimace the more reluctant man caught one wrist and reached for the other, twisting it behind his back. The fae cried out in agony, trying to clasp it back to his chest.

He was bleeding, didn't they see that? He was going to bleed out—

"Don't you worry." The first man lifted his chin with a smile. "We don't want any harm to come to you. We'll get you all fixed up." His smile widened as he tilted the prince's head, marveling at his face. "Can you understand what I'm saying? Do you speak the common tongue?"

Ellanden glared up at him, then let loose an oath so crazed and violent both men were convinced he spoke the common tongue after all.

"Gag him."

He struggled and twisted as a cloth was shoved between his teeth, but was in no condition to put up much of a fight. He hardly made a sound as he was lowered once again to the forest floor, bound and panting, little rivulets of blood streaming down the sides of his chest.

The man ripped open his shirt with a grimace. "Oh crap...you're lucky to be alive."

A pair of immortal eyes burned back at him.

"Yes, yes—I know. You want to kill me and all that." He gestured his friend forward, taking a roll of bandages from his hand. "Well, I'm sorry to disappoint you, sweetheart. But you're never going to get the chance."

With surprisingly efficient hands he removed the rest of the shirt and began looping the gauze around the fae's chest, packing some swiftly and carefully around the wound. There were several breathless cries as it was pressed into place, boots scrambling weakly against the leaves, but the prince's strength was spent. When the pain overwhelmed him he lay still upon the ground, eyes closed, secret tears vanishing into his ivory hair.

"I'll tell you what, though..." the man said as he hoisted him up against the tree, surveying him once again, "...you're going to make a pretty little slave. Fae are skilled with a blade, but they have other talents as well." He felt a lock of the prince's hair. "I'm sure we can get a fine price for you—"

"And what about me?"

Three pairs of eyes shot up at once as beautiful girl appeared in the clearing. She was battered, unarmed, and it looked like a small meteor had crashed into the side of her head.

But her hands were raised and her eyes were flaming.

The men stood up slowly, leaving the fae on the ground.

"And who might you be?" the taller of the two asked with a smile. Already his companion was moving in a slow circle away from them, coming at her from the other side.

Evie's hands were shaking, but she didn't back down.

"Get away from him," she said in a low voice. "*Now*."

Ellanden stared up at her from the ground. His eyes were screaming to run.

"Him?" The man gestured back with surprise, like he'd forgotten the fae was there. "We were just helping this young man. Apparently he got himself hurt in the forest. And what about you, my dear?" He took a step closer, eyes glittering in the light. "You look a bit undone yourself..."

She didn't wait for him to come any closer. She didn't wait for his companion to finish his circle and attack from the other side. A rush of dizziness crashed upon her, and before she could lose consciousness once again she took the only option still available to her.

She fired a wave of dragon fire from her hands.

The men died quickly, badly. She hardly noticed it herself, but the reflection of their writhing bodies was flickering in the fae's eyes. He tried to stand up, tried to reach her. But before he could make it to his knees, there was a violent trembling as the ground beneath them shook.

They were too close to the ravine. And there had been plenty of dragon fire to go around.

With twin cries the princess and the fae went flying over the side of the mountain, grabbing wildly onto rocks and tangles of shrubbery that were collapsing before their very eyes. What felt like a long time later, they finally spilled out onto the forest floor.

Neither was moving. Neither made a sound.

...are we dead?

The princess cracked open her eyes, one at a time. It was hard to make sense of anything. The world was tilted and her eyes were veiled with a sheen of blood.

"...Ellanden?"

The fae was lying not far from where she'd landed. One of his legs was still caught in a tree branch, tilting him gently towards the ground. His eyes blinked slowly open and shut, staring vacantly into the cloudless sky. The gag had ripped free and was hanging loose around his mouth.

"Ellanden," the princess tried again, lacking the strength to make it loud.

His head twisted weakly in her direction, a thin stream of blood trickling out of his mouth.

"Cada, si mios lyiona." He spoke in the language of the Fae, too disoriented to notice otherwise. His breath was quick and shallow, framing every word. "Cia…"

He reached a hand to the princess, though he could hardly tell who she was. Just another blurry figure. Brighter than the rest of the picture. Haloed in crimson swirls of hair.

And she wasn't the only one.

"Everly?"

A hush fell over the clearing as both of the friends froze very still. They couldn't tell if they were imagining it. Such a thing didn't seem real. The soft footsteps approaching, the gentle voice drifting lightly in the air. They lay in silence, looking dazed and hurt and very young, as another figure appeared above them. Another dazzling woman. Another swirl of crimson hair.

She reached down a hand to touch the princess' cheek.

"Oh, my poor darling."

It can't be…she's dead…

And yet there she was. Looking very much like the picture hanging in the corridor outside Evie's bedroom. The one she'd visit late at night, feeling around the edges, looking for adventure…

Adelaide Grey.

THE END

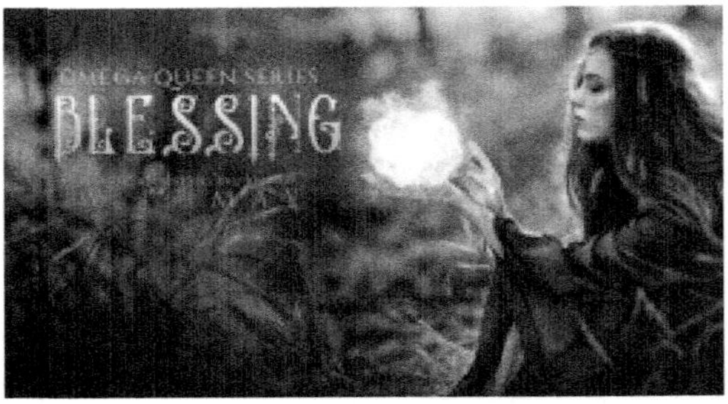
OMEGA QUEEN SERIES
BLESSING

Blessing Blurb

WHAT DO YOU SAY WHEN the dead come knocking...?

When an unexpected visitor shows up from the past, Evie's world flips upside-down. A long kept secret is forced into the open, as the enemy they've been racing is finally given a name.

Time is running out. But this quest isn't something they can do on their own.

Can they unite what's left of the five kingdoms? Can they fulfill the prophecy and find the missing stone in time? Or has their adventure been doomed to fail from the start?

Only time will tell...

The Queen's Alpha Series

Eternal
Everlasting
Unceasing
Evermore
Forever
Boundless
Prophecy
Protected
Foretelling
Revelation
Betrayal
Resolved

The Omega Queen Series

Discipline
Bravery
Courage
Conquer
Strength
Validation
Approval
Blessing
Balance
Grievance
Enchanted
Gratified

Find W.J. May

Website:
http://www.wjmaybooks.com
Facebook:
https://www.facebook.com/pages/Author-WJ-May-FAN-PAGE/141170442608149
Newsletter:
SIGN UP FOR W.J. May's Newsletter to find out about new releases, updates, cover reveals and even freebies!
http://eepurl.com/97aYf

More books by W.J. May

The Chronicles of Kerrigan

BOOK I - *Rae of Hope* is **FREE!**
Book Trailer:
http://www.youtube.com/watch?v=gILAwXxx8MU
Book II - *Dark Nebula*
Book Trailer:
http://www.youtube.com/watch?v=Ca24STi_bFM
Book III - *House of Cards*
Book IV - *Royal Tea*
Book V - *Under Fire*
Book VI - *End in Sight*
Book VII – *Hidden Darkness*
Book VIII – *Twisted Together*
Book IX – *Mark of Fate*
Book X – *Strength & Power*
Book XI – *Last One Standing*
BOOK XII – *Rae of Light*

PREQUEL –
Christmas Before the Magic
Question the Darkness
Into the Darkness
Fight the Darkness
Alone the Darkness
Lost the Darkness

SEQUEL –
    Matter of Time
    Time Piece
    Second Chance
    Glitch in Time
    Our Time
    Precious Time

Hidden Secrets Saga:
Download Seventh Mark part 1 For FREE
Book Trailer:
http://www.youtube.com/watch?v=Y-_vVYC1gvo

Like most teenagers, Rouge is trying to figure out who she is and what she wants to be. With little knowledge about her past, she has questions but has never tried to find the answers. Everything changes when she befriends a strangely intoxicating family. Siblings Grace and Michael, appear to have secrets which seem connected to Rouge. Her hunch is confirmed when a horrible incident occurs at an outdoor party. Rouge may be the only one who can find the answer.

An ancient journal, a Sioghra necklace and a special mark force life-altering decisions for a girl who grew up unprepared to fight for her life or others.

All secrets have a cost and Rouge's determination to find the truth can only lead to trouble...or something even more sinister.

RADIUM HALOS - THE SENSELESS SERIES
Book 1 is FREE

Everyone needs to be a hero at one point in their life.

The small town of Elliot Lake will never be the same again.

Caught in a sudden thunderstorm, Zoe, a high school senior from Elliot Lake, and five of her friends take shelter in an abandoned uranium mine. Over the next few days, Zoe's hearing sharpens drastically, beyond what any normal human being can detect. She tells her friends, only to learn that four others have an increased sense as well. Only Kieran, the new boy from Scotland, isn't affected.

Fashioning themselves into superheroes, the group tries to stop the strange occurrences happening in their little town. Muggings, break-ins, disappearances, and murder begin to hit too close to home. It leads the team to think someone knows about their secret - someone who wants them all dead.

An incredulous group of heroes. A traitor in the midst. Some dreams are written in blood.

Courage Runs Red
The Blood Red Series
Book 1 is FREE

WHAT IF COURAGE WAS your only option?

When Kallie lands a college interview with the city's new hot-shot police officer, she has no idea everything in her life is about to change. The detective is young, handsome and seems to have an unnatural ability to stop the increasing local crime rate. Detective Liam's particular interest in Kallie sends her heart and head stumbling over each other.

When a raging blood feud between vampires spills into her home, Kallie gets caught in the middle. Torn between love and family loyalty she must find the courage to fight what she fears the most and possibly risk everything, even if it means dying for those she loves.

Daughter of Darkness - Victoria
Only Death Could Stop Her Now
The Daughters of Darkness is a series of female heroines who may or may not know each other, but all have the same father, Vlad Montour. Victoria is a Hunter Vampire

HUNTRESS SERIES
USA TODAY BESTSELLING AUTHOR
W.J. MAY
LOOK BACK
MASTER
PERMISSION

PROPHECY SERIES
• W.J. MAY •
PROPHECY
• W.J. MAY •
PROPHECY
• W.J. MAY •
PROPHECY
• W.J. MAY •

The Chronicles of
KERRIGAN
W.J. May
RAE OF HOPE
DARK NEBULA
HOUSE OF CARDS
ROYAL TEA
UNDER FIRE
END IN SIGHT

THE HIDDEN
SECRETS SAGA
W.J. MAY

Don't miss out!

Visit the website below and you can sign up to receive emails whenever W.J. May publishes a new book. There's no charge and no obligation.

https://books2read.com/r/B-A-SSF-NJOIB

BOOKS 2 READ

Connecting independent readers to independent writers.

Did you love *Approval*? Then you should read *The Price For Peace*[1] by W.J. May!

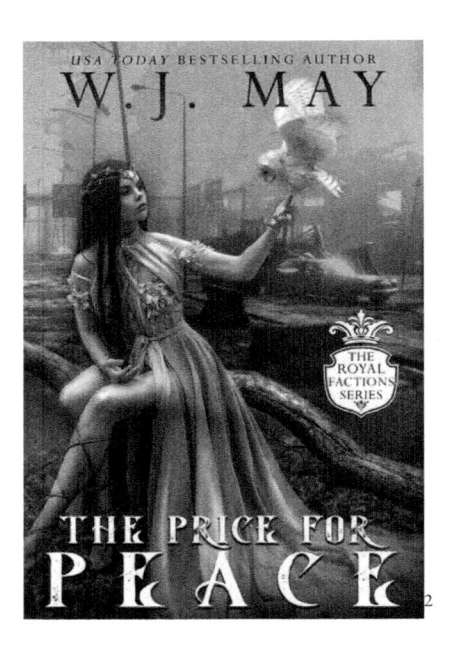

How do you keep fighting when you've already been claimed?

When sixteen-year-old Elise is ripped from her home and taken to the royal palace as a permanent 'guest', she thinks her life is over.

Little does she know it has only just begun...

After befriending a group of other captives, including the headstrong Will, Elise finds herself swept away to a world she never knew existed—polished, sculpted, and refined until she can hardly recognize her own reflection. She should be happy to have escaped the poverty of her former life. But she knows a dark truth.

The palace is a dream on the surface, but a nightmare underneath.

---

1. https://books2read.com/u/38EZXr

2. https://books2read.com/u/38EZXr

With a dwindling population, the royals have imprisoned the teenagers to marry and breed. Only seven days remain of freedom before they will be selected by a courtier and forever claimed.

Danger lurks around every corner. The only chance of escape is death.

But when the day of the claiming finally arrives...the world will never be the same.

Royal Factions
The Price for Peace – Book 1
The Cost for Surviving – Book 2
The Punishment for Deception – Book 3
Faking Perfection – Book 4
The Most Cherished – Book 5
The Strength to Endure – Book 6
Read more at www.wjmaybooks.com.

Also by W.J. May

Bit-Lit Series
Lost Vampire
Cost of Blood
Price of Death

Blood Red Series
Courage Runs Red
The Night Watch
Marked by Courage
Forever Night
The Other Side of Fear
Blood Red Box Set Books #1-5

Daughters of Darkness: Victoria's Journey
Victoria
Huntress
Coveted (A Vampire & Paranormal Romance)
Twisted
Daughter of Darkness - Victoria - Box Set

Great Temptation Series
The Devil's Footsteps
Heaven's Command
Mortals Surrender

Hidden Secrets Saga
Seventh Mark - Part 1
Seventh Mark - Part 2
Marked By Destiny
Compelled
Fate's Intervention
Chosen Three
The Hidden Secrets Saga: The Complete Series

Kerrigan Chronicles
Stopping Time
A Passage of Time
Ticking Clock
Secrets in Time
Time in the City
Ultimate Future

Mending Magic Series
Lost Souls
Illusion of Power
Challenging the Dark

Castle of Power
Limits of Magic
Protectors of Light

Omega Queen Series
Discipline
Bravery
Courage
Conquer
Strength
Validation
Approval
Blessing

Paranormal Huntress Series
Never Look Back
Coven Master
Alpha's Permission
Blood Bonding
Oracle of Nightmares
Shadows in the Night
Paranormal Huntress BOX SET

Prophecy Series
Only the Beginning
White Winter
Secrets of Destiny

Revamped Series
Hidden
Banished
Converted

Royal Factions
The Price For Peace
The Cost for Surviving
The Punishment For Deception
The Most Cherished
The Strength to Endure

The Chronicles of Kerrigan
Rae of Hope
Dark Nebula
House of Cards
Royal Tea
Under Fire
End in Sight
Hidden Darkness
Twisted Together
Mark of Fate
Strength & Power
Last One Standing
Rae of Light
The Chronicles of Kerrigan Box Set Books # 1 - 6

The Chronicles of Kerrigan: Gabriel
Living in the Past
Present For Today
Staring at the Future

The Chronicles of Kerrigan Prequel
Christmas Before the Magic
Question the Darkness
Into the Darkness
Fight the Darkness
Alone in the Darkness
Lost in Darkness
The Chronicles of Kerrigan Prequel Series Books #1-3

The Chronicles of Kerrigan Sequel
A Matter of Time
Time Piece
Second Chance
Glitch in Time
Our Time
Precious Time

The Hidden Secrets Saga
Seventh Mark (part 1 & 2)

The Kerrigan Kids
School of Potential
Myths & Magic
Kith & Kin
Playing With Power
Line of Ancestry
Descent of Hope
Illusion of Shadows
Frozen by the Future

The Queen's Alpha Series
Eternal
Everlasting
Unceasing
Evermore
Forever
Boundless
Prophecy
Protected
Foretelling
Revelation
Betrayal
Resolved
The Queen's Alpha Box Set

The Senseless Series
Radium Halos - Part 1
Radium Halos - Part 2

Nonsense
Perception
The Senseless - Box Set Books #1-4

Standalone
Shadow of Doubt (Part 1 & 2)
Five Shades of Fantasy
Zwarte Nevel
Shadow of Doubt - Part 1
Shadow of Doubt - Part 2
Four and a Half Shades of Fantasy
Dream Fighter
What Creeps in the Night
Forest of the Forbidden
Arcane Forest: A Fantasy Anthology
The First Fantasy Box Set

Watch for more at www.wjmaybooks.com.

About the Author

About W.J. May

Welcome to USA TODAY BESTSELLING author W.J. May's Page! SIGN UP for W.J. May's Newsletter to find out about new releases, updates, cover reveals and even freebies! http://eepurl.com/97aYf

Website: http://www.wjmaybooks.com

Facebook: http://www.facebook.com/pages/Author-WJ-May-FAN-PAGE/141170442608149?ref=hl *Please feel free to connect with me and share your comments. I love connecting with my readers.*

W.J. May grew up in the fruit belt of Ontario. Crazy-happy childhood, she always has had a vivid imagination and loads of energy. After her father passed away in 2008, from a six-year battle with cancer (which she still believes he won the fight against), she began to write again. A passion she'd loved for years, but realized life was too short to keep putting it off. She is a writer of Young Adult, Fantasy Fiction and where ever else her little muses take her.

Read more at www.wjmaybooks.com.

Printed in Great Britain
by Amazon